Angel's Trumpet

Angel's Trumpet

---

a novel by

Steve Cirrone

SFC Publishing
2022

ISBN:978-1-387-80334-7
Imprint: Lulu.com

***

for my husband
Charley Gilmore

PART ONE

ONE

I stand on a private balcony of this great ship overlooking small groups of people making their way across the deck below as night falls, the last night before the most difficult decision of my life.

A dirty vodka martini occupies my left hand, and I hold the chilled railing with my right hand. A cigarette burns itself in a nearby ashtray. It sends thin smoke into the salty air about me, and I am reminded of hours spent in similar company against the bar-rail behind where Colin eventually poured us away, drink after drink, the many hours I spent leaning, sometimes sitting, but always watching men come and go around me with the sunken, medicinal glances of West Hollywood, so wasted and routine. And what makes this unbearable to remember now is not the fact that these men exist—for they have always existed. No, what makes this unbearable is the fact that, no matter how I spend time in the company of others, no matter how many well-appointed rooms I have occasion to occupy, I will never be completely free of the despair I carry inside me equal to the sum of these men wherever I go.

If only I could let go.

The Mediterranean moves almost soundlessly to promise the sort of deep sleep that liquor poured steadily over ice can approach but never quite deliver. If I decide to push off here and now into that cold, dark water, it will surely take me into its quiet center to find stillness and silence. That deepness beckons the steel inside me to push through the gray and throw myself here and now over the side of this vessel to satisfy both God and man. The image of my body sinking into a perfect sleep flashes through my mind, but as much as I want to set my drink down and heave myself into the water, one thing, and one thing only, keeps me from moving to drown myself, and that is my cowardice—so I shrink away from what could very well have been my salvation, turn, and move to re-enter my cabin with a heavy irony, for it is cowardice that has led me here in the first place, to this very spot where lights below cast their glow upwards through the bottom of the glass that I still hold as the ice melts.

Maybe I will get drunk tonight, but that will do me little good. The alcohol would only weigh me down in its usual way and bring me no closer to action as the hours continue to pass as they must. The hours will pass and morning will come as surely as it always comes. And when morning comes, this great ship will dock, this movement will cease, and I will be forced in some way to deal with what has happened.

And how should I deal with it exactly?

I am still not sure, not sure at all. All I know is that, from this point onwards, no matter which way I choose to deal with it, I will have to keep my face very still, but this shouldn't be too difficult for someone like me, someone who has become accustomed to living life in tight places.

My given name is Davide Russo, pronounced Da-VEED ROO-so, but it's strange saying this name to myself, and I have no reason to do so. In grade school I suffered terribly for that final *e* in my Christian name because children, especially young boys, are cruel when it comes to singling out everything exceptional about one another. Many times I would suffer their brutality, especially on the playground, and this only served to highlight the ways in which I indeed differed from most of them. When I moved up into middle school, I dropped the *e* entirely and told everyone that my name had been officially changed to DAA-vid thinking the boys would stop harassing me so badly. The lie didn't work until those same boys began to talk in whispers and point in the hallways at girls who finally had their periods, and soon a great many of them seemed to care less and less about that final *e* and more and more about dawdling just outside the girls' locker room during gym class. Once the demands of puberty got the better of us, I've been David ever since, without the brutalizing *e,* and today only my parents continue to insist to use my given name whenever we have occasion to speak with each other, which isn't often. One time, as a senior in college, that year my seasonal boyfriend and I took nearly half a day to get to Staten Island on Thanksgiving, I said some words to get my parents to pronounce my name just like everyone else, but they just shook their heads at me and sat like sad dolls around the dining table with their mouths stitched shut.

I am tall, broad shouldered and attractive with my deep-set Sicilian eyes and browned skin. It is my attractive appearance that makes me someone people want to trust, I think, for it is natural to see goodness in beauty, and this has, for my entire life, certainly been a common misconception that I have worked to my advantage. And though I wouldn't say that I am a deceiver by nature, I think it fair to say that because people willingly deceive themselves, I have the advantage, when I would use it, to be naturally deceptive.

And then there is my outward disposition, an exterior I have worn with extraordinary precision on my current journey. Despite the reason for my being here, I have been able to exert an enormous amount of will, nearly all the will left in me, and the result has allowed me to walk in semblance around those on board, pulsing thick and darkly under a thin layer of someone else's skin. For the most part, I tell myself that I must play it safe and keep my palette dull, my words meaningless, inside a false cocoon of sorts, caught between what people see and what I can't yet admit. On deck, I have been a Hamlet, perhaps even a Lear, and successful in my role. The quick laughter I spent skirting between the Greek Isles and the Italian peninsula this past week has certainly misled my fellow sea-goers, has hood-winked them really. Perhaps I've fooled myself for a short time, posed inside this shroud as someone genuine, someone with a deep appreciation for all things wholesome with my dark, attractive Sicilian eyes, so round and deep-set.

But I am a liar.

Morning will come, and should I then decide to leave this sea and return to Los Angeles, I will fly seated next to passengers headed into the area on business, or for play. Most of these people will pass through the city unscathed and return home to familiar surroundings with pleasant memories of a full and fantastic place. A few passengers may be flying in to settle an old score, to begin a business venture, to oblige an aging relative, or perhaps, like I did just over a year ago, to attempt to force myself into its circumference and live there. I am not sure why so many people try to fit inside that demanding city—I am still not quite sure why I chose to live there. Perhaps some compulsion drew me to the city's core, the same compulsion that continues to draw others there, too. I would warn these people, if I could, to return to what they know, to embrace their place of origin and deny compulsion, for Los Angeles has given me only this nothingness. For all its tree-lined boulevards, for all its upscale, sugar-encrusted establishments, I have experienced the city's rotten core, have even contributed to it. I have known the rows upon rows of shadow-stretched alleyways that linger far from the angelic, have walked them all, a myriad of surreptitious channels conjoining towers of mirrored glass. So much cold fact, so much hard reflection should turn a soul inward, should lead a man to question his desires, not feed them recklessly. But I did feed them, we fed them together, Colin and me, and now here I am, far from what I knew to be my life, far from the life Colin and I shared too briefly in his small studio, there in that demanding city.

I suppose we succumbed to it together, each in his own way.

And should I get off this ship and on that plane, someone sitting next to me will surely talk to me, for someone always talks to me, about her upcoming affairs in the city, and she will ask, what brings me to that very spot? I will return to her a mechanical expression at most, for I won't be able to crack myself open and reveal the truth to her, of course. And so, I will curl the edges of my lips into a cold lie, exchange with her a few meaningless words, and then turn to search for a man in jeans sitting nearby. A blonde man. I have an unsettling penchant for fair-haired, light-eyed men. A blonde man. I will stare over the top of my rimless glasses at him for a while. I will watch the way he handles his drink, the way he excuses himself to step into the isle for the bathroom, the way he flips through the book he brought with him to pass the time. He will turn around at some point and catch me looking at him. He may smile at me. He may not. But he will be a blonde man.

Morning will come, and I will have to choose soon, but nothing good is sure to come of it. Do I return and subject this canvas to the streaks of shadow and light that await me, or do I bury my brush and drown my paints here in this sea forever, and cross a new current away from all that I have created to be my life? Or will some other method make itself known to me, a way to hold a full brush still for an endless amount of time over an eager canvas, an action that requires a will of the hand that may yet come to me here in this cabin that tosses itself lightly upon the sea? But I can't make such a decision, can't see clearly through this dull gray that overwhelms me to reach any conclusion. Not now, not tonight, for I am nearly drunk, and all I can do at this moment, here stumbling as

I am back towards the railing as the thick water moves below, is notice that the moon hasn't changed its place in the sky at all for what seems like hours. And then I'm leaning, holding with one hand gripping the railing, bending out over the side trying to find myself below in the sheen atop the water, extending my other arm out to touch its dark mirror, but I can see only the eddies swirl through the strata of water like layers and layers of time, and the entirety of the sea, so deep and tireless, murmurs over and over only that whatever I decide, steel or gray, my face must be still.

* * * * *

My stateroom is relatively tidy, and my belongings remain in their suitcase, aside from a few articles of clothing strewn about from the past few days and a tight picture of Colin and me on the nightstand obligatorily taken by a bored tourist passing by us during that first vacation together, on that long walk up and down South Beach while the sun moved overhead.

We look very happy in that photo.

I can see him on that day, tall, thin and glowing, on the day some tourist takes a picture of us with the sun overhead, his laugh erupting from him like a fountain, erupting like a fountain, fountain, every time we stop chatting to admire the summer heat reflected in the ripples rippling energetic people moving about us with the sun shining overhead. The waves cresting along the shore focus our attention away from the motley group of sun-bathers with their fit bathing suits and their tanned, sparkling skin. We laugh boldly there on the beach and walk a good half mile or so, laughing and meandering at times into the waterline that ebbs its way down the course of sand in front of us.

... he sometimes holds my hand as we pass the high-rise hotels, none of which we could truly afford, with their majesty overlooking the serene beach day. We walk until we see a cabana and then share a

cold drink as the wind catches our hair, throwing it into our eyes. Hair in our eyes and waves cresting the shore that lures Colin and me along in the sand, happy together in a photo ...

I met Colin in West Hollywood, on my 37th birthday. He walked into *Ici*, one of several nightclubs populating the corner of Santa Monica and Robertson. The moment I saw him, I knew it would end badly, but I didn't care; we were set into motion, perhaps for display, by some design far larger than either one of us could prevent from unfolding, even if we had desired it.

Despite the protections I kept erect and deliberate, the last few months had me feeling inordinately estranged from all life and activity in Los Angeles, including Rachel, and this dead distance created a hollowness that scratched inside me constantly, demanding that it be filled. And then Colin entered that night when I had been caged and given no choice but to pay close attention to him as the neon-lights overhead strained to distract us from our fate. But they were useless against his glow, and so it began, too late for both of us, as the final call for alcohol sent its anesthetizing warmth through our very veins.

The moment his form crossed my line of sight, a lifetime of watching men, watching their buttocks as they move themselves into a crowded room, watching their hands grasp hold of a beer bottle, watching their eyes as they flourish consonants in pen, turned a corner and became nothing to me. There would be no one else for me and no one else for Colin—I am sure he felt this way too, the moment we saw each other that night. I may be sure of few other things in this world, especially now, but this could not be more sure: there would be no one else for me and there would be no one else for Colin.

You see, it began too late for both of us.

As I stood with the curve of my lower back against the bar, my eyes locked on his form. Colin stepped across the room like a faun on thin glass, his energy spreading outward on a halo. I couldn't keep myself from eyeing his pulsing neck and his engorged lips as they worked to form and un-form words and expression, his facade hit me that hard. In that moment I also knew that there would be many nights ahead of me, nights loving Colin, holding him against me and feeling his skin rub raw against mine, our sweat mingling together and running into small pools on either side of our joined bodies as we made love over and over far into the morning, those nights with Colin, deep inside him, deep inside myself, being acted under an open sky, with no one and no thing to interfere with or slow the way in which our love making consumed each other so—but such was our undoing, for nothing is more unbearable, once one has it, than the desire to love and be loved. I suppose this is why Colin and I moved so quickly and so fully into each others' lives. I suppose this is why he, after three months, turned to me as the sun climbed over the Hollywood hills and told me he would love no other man but me, forever. That is the day I believed him, and today, even though he is no longer here to tell me these things, I choose to believe him still.

But life doesn't offer us the semblance of surety without a price, especially, as I came to know it, life in the City of Angels. The veneer city swirls as furtive as the sea, overreaching and ever deep, it tangos the complacent moon and the eager shore, and it refuses to keep anything close to us for long—ripples rippling energy the breakwater overreaching us pulling us under, pulling us deep. It gives and takes, without cause or justification, and the greatest difficulty is to struggle atop the water as the waves come, grasping into eddies, until the tide washes lovers and friends and life and living itself away with yesterday's sand.

* * * * *

One thing I regret—for all the good it does me now—is the lie I retold so often that I believed it, the lie I told Colin soon after we met. I told him that I never loved anyone before, but that is not the truth. I never told Colin about Gabriel.

Seeing Colin enter that first night brought Gabriel into my throat, thick and smoky. Seeing Colin that first night should have made me choke on Gabriel, but instead, I swallowed hard and continued to ogle the prize in front of me.

I hadn't thought about Gabriel much over the past year in Los Angeles, having deliberately moved him out of my immediate thoughts and replacing his memory with an abundance of work and a variety of meaningless sexual encounters. And after my gaze fixed on Colin and remained there as days stretched into months, I pushed Gabriel into a corner of my mind so remote to lose him there, but despite my efforts, at times—like the first time I saw Colin, like the night I left Colin, and like tonight on this balcony—Gabriel comes easy enough, pressing my bones to fire as only his ghost could, and I have to question whether or not my choices have indeed been as deliberate and as careful as I would have them be.

When I began to love Gabriel, it was the start of summer, an Atlanta summer, and that meant the air was thick and hot. Atlanta summers hang thick and hot, with the air itself heavy on the tongue. I had just finished giving a final exam to one of my college composition classes. Gabriel was one of my students, and a constant source of anxiety for me the entire semester. His writing was terrible, riddled with sentence errors and poor diction, but I did not care. His pale blue eyes, untroubled by complexity, paired themselves against his nearly translucent skin. His skin was angelic, I suppose. He was deceptively graceful, too, and it was painfully clear to me, each time he moved, that I had to touch him, to enter his thin frame, to stake his heart through and make him mine. I knew these desires were wrong, that Gabriel, so much younger than me, so ignorant of the predatory ways of men especially, and a pupil of mine, should have been off-limits to me. Like a ripe apple on a neighbor's tree, he should have been one out of reach. But that knowledge, too, did not keep me from looking boldly into his blue eyes as he turned in his last hastily written essay to round out a semester of subpar academic performance. I looked into his blue eyes then and asked him to pass the afternoon with me.

We passed a few hours at a café in Midtown revisiting some of the material we had covered that term in class. Gabriel sat across from me, dressed in gym-casual clothes that did much to accentuate his lithe form, and he spent much of our conversation fixated on his tongue piercing, showing it off to me as some sort of trophy, giving me opportunities to imagine what it would feel like inside my mouth and then, mucous-rich, rubbed along the head of my penis. With so much distraction, I tried to keep the conversation academic in scope, but my eyes gave me away. Soon he very clearly saw me for what I was and recognized what it was I wanted from him, and I was somewhat surprised when he did not offer any protest. Just as the sun began to set, we took leave from the café and made our way in separate cars to my house on 8th, and when he agreed to stay that night, I was overjoyed.

For a while, we passed time indoors talking about inane topics—clothing, popular club music, television programs—any topic on which he could hold an opinion. Our conversation took us well into the evening, and we ordered some Chinese food from the corner kitchen which made us laugh and use chopsticks poorly. And then I put in one of my favorite movies, *La Passion de Jeanne d'Arc*, so that I could share Dreyer's genius and Falconetti's immortal performance with him—but as much as I wanted him to enjoy the film in exactly the way I would have him enjoy it, we weren't really watching it. At least I know I wasn't. Oh, my face spent much of the time directed at the screen in front of us, but my mind raced alongside my heart for nearly an hour until I steeled myself to reach for his large white hand—so masculine in shape yet delicate in touch—and hold it in mine. The rest of the movie faded into lost sound and blurred movement as we looked deeply for the first time into each other's eyes—such happiness I saw reflected there! In that moment all was right with heaven, for Gabriel loved me then, and the world was perfectly pure and perfectly good, holding Gabriel's white hand.

Within a few weeks, Gabriel moved himself fully into my house with an abundance of hip clothes and a stack of half-read schoolbooks, and despite a few boxes of his other belongings which we crammed in the back of the guest room closet, we very soon came to occupy the thousand square feet of space in easy concert. Weeks passed quickly, as if time itself surrendered to the gravity of our closeness, and we rarely argued and never about anything substantial. At times, we forced some heated exchanges—some hot words over innocuous household matters like the type of toothpaste we should use or the time we should start dinner—just for the sake of getting ourselves irritated so that our lovemaking would benefit from the friction, but even then Gabriel remained perfect because he didn't demand anything from me once the exchange and our lovemaking ended. He never asked to move a piece of furniture because he didn't care for its location or to paint a room a different color because he couldn't agree with its hue. He adjusted himself into the routine of my life without complaint, and he not once pressed his will against my own—he didn't have to, for he slipped into my life without discord, and once he resonated inside the space I opened for him, it was as if he had always been there, submissive and sanctified.

We did spend a considerable amount of time, however, focused on improving the outside of my house, but these were improvements that I had been putting off or fully neglecting, so I was grateful for his assistance. One weekend, we painted the eaves that lined my roof. We painted the underside of the eaves white and the visible cross- and eye-beams black so they would really pop against the Dutch Blue exterior color and dark shale roof tile. It took us the majority of both Saturday and Sunday to complete the task, and a lot of time was spent going up and down ladders while juggling paint-cans and paintbrushes, but when the job was finished I couldn't help but remark on the improvement it made to the curb appeal of my home, and I was pleased with the result. I wouldn't have had the motivation to labor so without Gabriel.

Outside activities also took place in my garden. I remember vividly the first Sunday we spent an entire afternoon on our knees in the dirt tending to the patch of overlooked ground that grew wild along the north side of my bungalow. I had let it fester for far too long, in truth I had fully neglected it for several seasons, and now an unruly assortment of half-rotted blooms, uneven clusters of long and multi-colored grasses and an unkempt puzzle of flowering vines spread themselves without restriction across the entire bed, making it so discordant that only a great effort could harmonize the space again. I remember how it took us an entire day, from dawn to dusk, for Gabriel and me to trim it all back and bring it together into some semblance of order. We worked the two of us up and down the space hardly exchanging any words at all, snipping and gathering, plucking and trashing, with only our conjoined spirits to guide us, for we understood what had to be done to improve the space without actually having to discuss it out loud, we were that much in tune with one another. And once the garden had been improved by our care, we continued to tend to it whenever we found ourselves near its region of earth, pulling weeds as soon as they appeared, removing fallen leaves to prevent choking new and wanted growth, and cutting long- and short-stemmed flowers when necessary that we used to brighten the bay window in the kitchen. Gabriel came into my life and brought with him an ease of companionship I had never known before. It was if I was able to breathe easier because I knew that he would be close at hand, receptive and genuine, and if my days and nights seemed complete it was only because of him.

Without doubt, I had loved Gabriel.

He was killed six months later while walking home from a local club that one night I decided I was too tired and annoyed to accompany him out dancing and drinking. We had argued childishly about it, called each other silly names, and then I let him go out into the night. Just a few blocks away from where I lay in bed waiting for him to return to me, he bled to death and died while I lay in bed alone without him to return to me because I was too tired and too annoyed to accompany him. I didn't know what had happened to him for two whole days, two terrible days that found me sitting at home having nothing to do with my hands, alone, unable to think clearly or think about anything else except keeping my hands in awkward uselessness. No one called me to let me know he had been killed. A day or so later, I learned about the hit-and-run death of a young man on the local news, and the very moment I heard about this death, the outside world suddenly tightened against my skin, and I knew Gabriel was dead, that I would never see his eyes open to me again, and that I would live and die alone because I had loved him too much to accompany him after an argument.

The world no longer made sense to me, its recognizable colors now fused into gray, and I couldn't engage a foot or an arm to get out of bed for what seemed like days, but I am sure I must have gotten up to use the toilet at some point or to get another pack of cigarettes from where I kept them from Gabriel under some unused sweaters piled on the top shelf of the linen closet. That must have been when the phone rang, again, and I decided to pick it up instead of letting it go to voicemail as it had been doing for hours or days.

"It's about time."

I recognized the voice right away. It was Rachel, one of two women I knew who gave me pause since my arrival in Atlanta five years previous. The first woman to do this was Cheryl, a woman with a walk that seduced me nearly, a woman so elegant and glittering that when she moved into a room the furniture yearned. I have no idea where Cheryl is today, and I haven't thought about her in many years, having pushed aside the notion of completeness with a woman, as complete as she was. And then Rachel, with her soft mulatto hair and eyes, with her frank smile and her solid calves, came into my life a short time after Cheryl left it, and for some reason, what discouraged Cheryl only drew from Rachel endearment.

"David—why haven't you been answering your phone? Or your door?"

"You've knocked on the door?"

"A million times!"

"I'm sorry."

"Don't be ridiculous," she said quietly into the phone.

"I suppose I am being ridiculous, aren't I?"

"No, no," Rachel replied, "Not at all. That's not what I meant at all."

"Listen, Rachel, I should . . ."

"David, I know. I heard. Is there anything I can do for you, David? Do you need anything?"

"You—heard?"

"Yes."

"How did you hear?"

Rachel sighed real slowly.

"Chris called me this morning, he was home watching the news, and, well, there it was—on the news. His name, his picture. All of it. I'm so sorry, David."

"Yes."

I looked around the room where I sat, still in bed. Gabriel filled the very air around me—as if he stood just there, or just there. And the more I sensed him in the space around me, the more segments of our life together pinched me deeper into the creases of the mattress under my back. The small television we rescued from his parents' house stood on top of my dresser; an old pack of his Marlboro Lights lay half crumpled on top of my desk next to his laptop which was perpetually signed into Facebook—a dozen open windows flashed waiting for his response; his watch, the silver one with the green dial that I gave him for Christmas last year, ticked away the time right beside me on the nightstand; and a small pile of rejected party clothes lay on the chair where he had left them just before he walked out the door into the darkness and his death. I smelled him everywhere, too, of course, his own sweet scent, and Gabriel always smelled good. And if I closed my eyes, then my ears would begin to trick me as I heard him walking heavy-footed throughout the front of the house, and all of it—all of it—began to shut me down completely. I knew that the memory of my love for Gabriel would continue to press me until madness came, until wretchedness claimed every part of my manhood taking with it my will to leave the small space. Despair began to fill me then, and a cavern of black so remote, so lonesome, opened inside me. It sent all the blood from my face into the pit of my stomach, making me dizzy and causing my hands to tremble. Deep in my mind, as if displayed upon a remote cavern wall, I could see only desperate and obscene images flicker and move inside a small ring of jagged stone, and I became even more afraid. I saw my life end there as surely as I have ever seen anything.

And then, in that moment, in that very moment, I made a decision.

"Rachel, I need to get out of here."

"Okay, I'll be right there. I'm already walking to the car—you wait for me David. We'll take a drive to the coast for . . ."

"No, I mean, I need to leave this city. I can't stay here, stay in here, anymore. It's . . . it's going to be too hard."

"Where would you like to go?"

"Someplace else, someplace warm," and then, "California."

Rachel was quiet for only a moment.

"Fine. That's fine. I'll go with you."

"You'll . . . go?"

"Yes. I'll go with you. Just tell me when."

"I can't make you do that."

"Who's making me? I want to go with you."

"What about Chris?"

"Oh, please. Chris," she sighed. "Really, I've had it with him. He'll never change, that Chris. I'm tired of waiting around expecting him to suddenly be the person he told me he was when we first met." And then, after a short pause, she continued. "This is a good thing, David, the two of us going to California. You'll see, it'll be a new start for both of us."

And then, for some reason, I laughed. I can't remember exactly why I laughed, but I do remember the sound of it coming out of my mouth and rebounding off the walls to fill my ears. It was a curious sound in that fortress of misery, but I let the sound come nonetheless, and I laughed. If my sudden outburst disturbed Rachel, she certainly didn't let on to it. In fact, she remained quiet on the other end of the line—she was probably waiting for me to continue to protest her willingness to leave her life behind and follow me. But I didn't say a thing because I knew she was right. Chris was not the man for her, anyone could see that, and I didn't want to lose myself forever chained inside the dark cavern opening in my mind. Whatever living left within us needed to be dug out, needed to be scraped from under dead rock and exposed to a new slant of light.

Had I known then that my decision to move to California would bring with it an even greater misery—the misery I carry with me here on this ship, the misery I will carry with me until my death—I would have stopped and stayed in that house. I would have let the devil of that darkness brick me in to die there and been more at peace with the world and myself for having done so.

Instead, I laughed.

I don't even remember saying goodbye before the phone was no longer up to my ear. It was back where it had been, on the nightstand, face down, and I was up from bed and in the shower. Then came water on my skin. Hot water, hotter than most showers I've taken. I remember scrubbing my skin very hard and staying under the hot water until my fingertips began to crease and fold. I washed my hair over and over with creased fingertips, and the lingering smell of all those cigarettes began to disappear as the foam ran down my legs into the drain below my feet.

Once I felt I was clean enough to step from the water, I dressed quickly, determined to leave Atlanta as soon as possible, and that meant that very day or the next, if possible. I took stock of what was left around me. I needed only some clothing and my laptop—everything else I would leave behind for it would have served to remind me of Gabriel, and that would not be good for me or for anyone where I was going. I even threw away all the pictures we took together, save one, a black and white photo of him holding Macie, our pet retriever. I suddenly thought of that dog and how the poor animal had mysteriously run away a few weeks ago. I had cried for nearly two days over her disappearance, and that, too, no longer seemed to matter. I left all my things behind because I wanted to leave Georgia completely and as soon as possible, and nothing else seemed to matter.

The house would have to be sold, of course, but I was sure my friend Anna, she was a Good Anna, who had sold the house to me in the first place, would market the dwelling without my having to physically be here. She was very good at her job, this Good Anna, and she worked herself nearly to death shuffling clients about at all hours of the day and night, but she had a beautifully crested home in Druid Hills, three other properties across the city that she rented out for extra income, and two foreign cars to show for her trouble. She had no man in her life. It was good to know that Anna would work to sell the house because I would certainly need some money to start over in Los Angeles—that is where I would go, then.

I suppose that was when I decided I would move to Los Angeles, in that very moment when I thought about Good Anna and the house having to be sold, and that was when I began this flight into my ever-deeper misery, a flight which would bring me to lean against this brass rail under a darkened Mediterranean sky.

And yet, as I consider now more carefully what decision exactly led to this present, exactly which moment behind led to that one in front, I cannot seem to sound its course. Instead, I relax my grip on the railing a bit and stare out across the water to try and listen to what it is telling me. I strain but hear nothing that I can make out clearly, and still I stare and stare. Perhaps it is the mystery of the sea that keeps me entranced so, but I begin to wonder about all those cross-currents—how they must create watery restrictions for all the life below. I close my eyes, and I imagine myself surrounded by a ring of luminescent seahorses that desire to school untamed; these delicate creatures will not allow themselves to be reined. They encircle me, faster and faster, darting closer and closer from every corner of the balcony and from inside the stateroom, even from inside the photo that lords over the whole of the cabin from its place on the nightstand. Caught, I realize that my flight only seemed to begin the moment I decided to entrust the house to Good Anna and move to Los Angeles with Rachel in tow. That which propelled me to make such a decision, well, that had been stirring my blood for as long as I could remember.

* * * * *

I continue to listen to the sound of the water lapping against the hull of the ship, and my mind fills with thoughts of Staten Island where I was raised, and where my parents now live in separate houses, only a few miles apart. I have been on my own ever since I went upstate to college, the only time in my life that I recall with a sense of longing because I knew myself well then. During those college years, I had the kind of confidence that bordered on conceit, but this conceit grew in me with good reason. I excelled in all my studies, finding it hard to choose where to spend my energy. Drawing, mathematics, writing, chemistry—all came easy to me, as I had always known it would. Ever since I was very little, I learned that nothing would challenge me into frustration. I just wouldn't let it.

I was born with an adaptable intelligence, my mother used to say. Somehow I think this had everything to do with my being attracted to boys and, later, to men. And later still, to Colin. The most sincere attraction of one man to another can only be borne of adaptable intelligence.

While I was away up at school, my sister Annie would call me every now and then to tell me that my parents were getting along badly, and without ever knowing how or why I felt it, I felt that their long battle had everything to do with me, with me being homosexual. The last time I went home, right after I graduated from college, I came right out and told them about my circumstances and that I was going to move even further away, attend a graduate program in Atlanta, and live with a young, stout German named Samuel. I could see in their faces the sheer disappointment I had brought into their lives after so many years of expectation—there would be no toast of champagne after the expense of a traditional wedding and no grandchildren. There would be no mousy woman to help my mother and sister set the holiday table, and there would be no grandchildren. We didn't discuss my move away, my shift in perspective, further that day or for many days afterwards, and only now, many years later, many years after their marriage fell first into silent blaming and then fell away, many years after I followed whatever path had been opened before me by turning away from them and their unhappiness, can I say with any surety that my parents have lost some of their disappointment—or perhaps they have just given up wishing circumstances were different.

But at twenty-one, I wanted nothing more than to be free of my parents' long faces that pressed into me like stones. So I left to live my life the way I thought it should be lived, and I have never truly looked back; and when a teaching position opened up at a local community college just north of Atlanta, long after my relationship with Samuel had ended, I took it to get ahead in my career because I knew that it was right for me. And I was just as sure, on the day I finally answered the phone when Rachel called, that leaving Gabriel to be buried by his parents and moving to Los Angeles was right for me, for *me*, for I have always been selfish.

For I am—or I was—one of those people who pride themselves on their ability to mistake selfishness for opportunity, to seize the moment as it is given without thought for others or for the interconnectedness of the world as it spins around me, to rise, to fulfill whatever promise I believed I had and never to yield. In this way, I was made to eventually live in a city like Los Angeles, I suppose, a place that would add its layers to me and fill me out, grotesquely. I genuinely believed that by moving far away, yet again, I would be able to hold the content of my life up to even the most demanding scrutiny, parental or otherwise. I would be able to point to just this or just that in the stream of accomplishments that make up the current of my life and say, "see here how I have exceeded your mark," and "see there how I have created something beautiful." Yes, by moving away—away from New York, away from Georgia—I would be my own initiator, my own manager, or so I believed.

But I have learned differently.

I have learned that people who are good at taking what is given to them and who therefore believe themselves to be masters of their own destiny can only continue to believe this by becoming artful in self-deception. This evening, now in the square mirror atop the vanity in the stateroom, I face myself, perhaps for the first time honestly, and the barren expression I see there tells me that there is no greater artist. As I continue to stare at the steel-edged form reflected before me, I come to understand that I must have been operating with a kind of blindness, and that my decisions could not have been real decisions at all—for none of my decisions have ever brought me closer to humility. I see now that all has been an elaborate and false creation: running away with Samuel to avoid seeing my parents' marriage fall apart; escaping to Los Angeles instead of braving Gabriel's parents and properly burying my lover in Atlanta—and my being here on this ship—these and like decisions, all designed to make the world appear to be what they and the world are not. And now, all I have to show for my life is this chain of evasions that hangs about my neck, an albatross.

This is certainly what my decision to leave New York came to, made so long ago. To run, and to keep running with eyes and throat pressed forward, so as to allow no opening for shame or doubt, for a life like mine can't be lived otherwise.

I succeeded very well at first. I didn't allow myself to feel or to accept blame for the hurt I caused others. I turned away from it all by staying in constant motion, like this ship itself, in order to avoid looking at myself fully through a static piece of the day or night framed around me, and as a result, I became unbending and hard. And if I felt myself losing hold of my will, if I felt my stare turn towards the mirror without candles or the moon, the bottle came quickly into my hand and I would lose myself in careless orgies until self-doubt passed on the backs of seahorses once again.

It came as no surprise then, really, that on the day Colin died, I got on a plane, and then on this vessel, but I think I knew, in the very center of my being, exactly what I was doing when I took this boat for the sea.

TWO

As I have already confessed, I met Colin on my birthday near the start of my second year in Los Angeles, not too long after I was given a tenure-track position at the college where I had been teaching since moving out west, so money was available again. The house in Atlanta had recently sold too, thanks to the Good Anna, and I carelessly began to frequent the West Hollywood bars that spread their anesthesia from the city center.

I enjoyed the quiet for the most part, safe with Rachel close by, still too raw to extend genuine feeling towards anyone or any group of people, despite *le milieu* trying to claim me as part of its entourage. But the more such people tried to pull me into their circles, their dirty, often promiscuous circles, the more I managed to sidestep them all, as if I was intent on proving, to them and to myself, that I was not of their company. I wanted to stay just out of reach, especially so because I was now a widower of sorts, a wronged man. I was a person who had suffered for love, a person who continued to suffer, and my suffering made me someone difficult to hold let alone hold fast.

I suppose this was when I began to realize that I was defined, contained even, by a combination of will and circumstance that kept me removed from everything and everyone that circled and circled in patterns around me in the patterns of vultures circling, and it didn't take long for a sort of manufactured piety to settle on me, reflected in all the black little eyes. And in a place like West Hollywood, a place where black little eyes dot vanquished souls, just about everyone who did set their black little eyes on me appeared only more sinister and decayed for doing so, and this served to push me further from their talons, inviolate and inconsumable. For nearly a year, up until the moment I saw Colin, up until the very moment his halo extended across *Ici* to where I sat caged at the bar, whenever someone other than Rachel tried to embrace me sincerely in even the slightest of ways—asking for some way to contact me again, asking to see me again someplace other than in the place I stood, asking to see me again after a night of meaningless sexual contact—a barrier went up around me that sent every offending tongue and limb recoiling to the highest distance, and I became more and more attractive simply because I became more and more of an enigma.

Now, as I sit in my stateroom staring out across the sea, I could wish that I had kept myself inside the fortress I built for myself, safe from the seduction of the city-slick fingers that reach up inside a shirt and squeeze the blood so completely from every passageway around a heart. I could wish that I kept myself protected inside that fortress I created for myself for just a day longer—an hour even—and so much would not be the way it is now.

But, as I said, it was the night of my 37th birthday, and Rachel had insisted that we eat at one of those pricy restaurants and that we then spend some time going from bar to bar up and down the Boulevard in search of something that would take my mind off the misery of the past and make me happy for an evening. And I—I dared to go off into the night in search of that very thing.

* * * * *

After dinner, I took Rachel to make a calculated appearance at *Ici*, an establishment that used to be something else entirely, when the corner of Robertson and Santa Monica was more still and the *soiree* didn't demand yet more vanity pumping through the aorta of West Hollywood. I imagine that the world without *Ici* would be quiet, but now the heart runs through everything.

As we entered I remarked on how the bar seemed more than ordinarily crowded for a weekday night. By the time we arrived, all the fixtures had taken their usual places in dark corners to begin the night's long routine of sending black little eyes at each other across safe distance. In the open spaces, men milled about the club *en masse* though some packed themselves deliberately into clusters to interfere with the demands of regular travel. In one spot, a group in expensive business attire made disinterested conversation across the tops of their rock glasses; they shared dull remarks, as was their custom, on the state of the economy and how it had affected the business of the city. In another, a few pairs of leather chaps shifted their moustaches around a pitcher of beer, exchanging jabs meant to penetrate isolation and hold back despair; and in front of the mirrored wall, a group of tank-tops calculated gin and tonics as they attempted to surreptitiously measure the breadth and weight of their reflections against one another. And then there were the four elegant looking Versace queens pressed around a small center bar table. They conversed in an animated manner designed to attract as much attention as possible because not one of them would ever attract much attention by himself. Still they sipped on their neon pink Cosmopolitans with a deliberate and mutually agreed upon insistence, surrounded by innumerable pairs of black little eyes more interested in catching glimpses of the collection of knife-blade lean, tight-jeaned boys going round and round. These boys all knew each other, had probably slept with each other on nights when lack of rotation clouded their minds, or when pangs of desire sharply rose the inoculating conviction that they, too, should try to find a living person to hold them until dawn broke the horizon. Yes, all the regulars were at the bar that night, and they moved or stood still, all with something behind their eyes at once terribly vulnerable and terribly hard.

As we pushed our way into the room, Rachel and I were aware, we were both very much aware, that we had suddenly become the focus of the entire establishment's motley and sordid attention as everyone watched us enter, and for a moment it felt like we had unwittingly trooped onto a battleground where all the guns had silencers, and all the shadows held an army of marksmen, and all their black little eyes targeted me for Rachel was not significant here. The onslaught of so many eyes digging themselves into my calves and shoulder-blades gave me a certain degree of pleasure, I admit, for nothing works so well to erase a man's doubt than the focused admiration of a host of unknowns—especially if it promises danger and lasts five minutes.

My attractive, dark Sicilian eyes and skin.

After a short time, we found ourselves near a bar station and were able to order our staple cocktails, and soon the guy behind the bar began to hit on me in a non-committal sort of way, which is what bartenders are supposed to do here in this place, I suppose. Maybe it was the alcohol, or the fact that it was my birthday, but this flirting came at me hard; it made me grip and spin around on my stool with a smile on my face—a smile!—and that's when I saw him, the faun—the most delicate, the most demure creature I had ever seen since Gabriel. I had loved Gabriel. He came half-through the entranceway laughing that fountain laugh of his that erupted like a fountain that I would soon get to know too well. His loose blonde thick curls bounced around and behind his earlobes giving him the look of a Norse god or a French king. His large, mystical eyes opened as large as saucers, and his skin so white and clear made him appear sculpted from a refined and purged marble. For a moment he stopped short in the doorway with a sudden look of hesitation on his face—hesitation, he stopped short in the doorway.

Colin hesitated.

And why wouldn't he hesitate? A gazelle at the entrance of a den of hungry wolves should do more than pause; it should turn and run. But then, whatever gave him pause, whatever reared up in warning and kicked its front legs out against the danger of this hard and dark place, just as quickly as it appeared, the look of hesitation left him. He hesitated only a moment, the look left him, and then he stepped into the den and he entered the den and he entered.

"Time to move," Rachel said, suddenly at my elbow. "Here comes Justin. Oh, goddamn it all, too late. He's seen us."

"*Daaa*vid!

Justin's voice was unmistakable, its high pitch straddled all chatter around it pushing it down into the murk, and I turned to see someone who barely passed for a man waving a hand high in the air at me from the other side of the crowded room. Before long, the hand fell limp and he came closer and closer still. He walked on his toes, his flat hips moved nearly grotesquely in time with the low tones of the background music. As he traveled toward me, he seemed to make no sound; all I could hear was Colin's fountain laugh buoyed by the ebb and echo of bar conversations which rushed past me like the sea at night. As he continued to move towards me, I could see the particles rise off Justin to glitter in the dim light; the thin hair looked sharp and wet, hung low across his forehead, the eyelids and cheeks dusted with a fine powder. And when he finally stopped directly in front of me, I could smell his familiar gardenia rising out of the neckline even before he parted his mouth raged with a deep-colored lipstick. Then he moved closer, close enough for me to see the sunken tracks of many years of pills running parallel down either side of his face, and I could feel him nearly on top of me, breathing and breathless. A red sash hung loosely around his waist, and the pants clung tight and gray to his form. He wore rhinestone buckles on his shoes.

"My, my, my," Justin began, keeping his voice high and deliberate. "David, is that *really* you? You'd better be careful, people might think you're trendy like the rest of us. Can't have you fall *all* the way, you know. Getting back up again is murder—I should know, love, I've fallen down and risen back up again so many times now, I'm, well, stuck in a wicked soufflé that someone else just bakes over and over *eternellement*."

"Hello, Justin. How have you been?"

"Oh you know old queens, we are always the same," he replied, as he sipped hard on some fruit-flavored alcoholic beverage through a thin, red straw. He looked absently around the bar before continuing. "Ah well. The crows and the chickens are flapping their wings in full measure tonight. Any feather interesting to pluck in this coup? Besides you, of course."

"There is now," Rachel said dryly.

Justin turned towards her and then garishly twisted his face into an expression one makes when unexpectedly tasting something dreadfully sour. "I see you brought *it* with you, stuck to your side like a cancerous tumor, as always."

"That's not fair, Justin. You know very well that Rachel is the only constant in my life. I wouldn't go anywhere without her."

"Well, you could *try*, David, really, and give one of us poor enamored bastards the chance to shamelessly throw ourselves at you without having to wrestle with—*it*," Justin peered again around the room, his tongue on his straw, and then let his eyes fall directly on Rachel. "Besides, doesn't it get tired being the old maid all the time?"

"Oh I don't know, Justin," Rachel said. She drew her small, thin fingers through her long, dark hair lifting it off from around her face and reaffixing it with the fancy pin she liked to wear whenever we went out together. "You never seem to grow tired of it."

I felt the sides of my mouth curl up as I let out a reflexive laugh and turned my face away before I made Justin feel terrible about himself, but the chatter around us had evaporated momentarily and he heard me without cover.

"Go on, David, let it all out, lover—one day, when I'm no longer here to adore you because someone younger and more attractive . . . just stepped onto the bus looking for an inviting place to sit down . . . trust me, you'll miss me, and so terribly, too, that you will suffer horrible pain, here." He pointed to my head. "And here," he said with a finger at my heart. "And most definitely, here," he said with a plump, small hand moving towards my genitals.

"No doubt, Justin," I said as I caught his hand in mid-air.

"Hmph," Justin turned around to walk away but stopped suddenly and turned back to me, "All this open hostility nearly made me forget why I risked being eaten alive by your hag in the first place." Justin fumbled around in his back pocket for a bit and withdrew two neatly folded pieces of paper. "Here!"

I looked down at the thick paper being forced into my hand. It sparkled.

"What is it?"

"Well, you *can* read, can't you? I swear, the more attractive, the more lazy, truly—this entire city is full of the likes of you, David. Sling, sling, bring me a sling! It's getting as bad as Avon calling around here," Justin deliberately raised his voice even higher above the surrounding noise. "It's an invitation to my new opening."

"Opening?"

"I'm coordinating an AIDS benefit."

"Oh."

"Now, now, now. It won't be glum! We have wonderful drugs these days—keeps a mummified corpse upright and barely functioning for years. Just like Reagan during his second term, irony of ironies. Proof positive God has a wicked sense of humor. You will come, won't you? Friday night, at *Cirque Fantastique*. That pass is good for two, so if you must, you can bring *it* with you, I suppose."

The music changed slightly, increasing in intensity and volume a bit, and a heavy beat, thick with artificial drums thumping below waves of harmonious pipe fugues began to reverberate the air and pulse against the many conversations still filling the space around us. From above, rays of thick red and a more translucent blue began to crisscross the air at sharp angles. The shift indicated it was nearly 1 A.M., and the energy in the club took on a pronounced dimension of anxiety; some of the people took the change in music as a sign to begin to quit the space for home, but for those who remained it was as if an engine moved with some effort into overdrive. The well-groomed Versace queens by the front entrance pressed even closer around their martini fortified cocktail table, their discordant voice shrilled ever higher; some desperate, smack-thin hustlers still lacking johns began to lean more provocatively against one another; the three bartenders adjusted themselves with thick fingers deliberately hoping to lure a final school of tips through the steady bait and business of last call; and all the while the bar-backs charged through the thinning crowd gathering empty glasses in order to prepare the space for as early a departure as possible.

The shadows of half-empty shells of creatures more akin to piranha than men began to bleed their distinctive colors from every corner to threaten the balance of the entire room.

Somehow I had lost sight of the faun.

“Oh, it looks like I pulled two of these from my pocket—so, handsome, it looks like you get one too!” Justin said loudly as he reached past me to the left and handed one of his sparkling invitations to someone standing behind me. When he did, he leaned into me, and with a strange, almost benevolent look on his face whispered directly into my ear, “Remember what I said, David. This city is awfully fickle, cruel even—the wheel’s gotta spin, kiddo, and no one rides for free. *Adieu mon chere.*” When Justin stepped back, his face took on its accustomed expression of disinterest, and after announcing with a flourish that he had to leave us to make last rounds, he withdrew back into the crowd and was gone. His red sash and red lipstick and rhinestone buckles fell back into the crowd, and the crowd and its dark center swallowed him whole, and he was gone.

“Good god, he is such a *queen*,” Rachel scoffed as she rolled a piece of ice around in her mouth. “How does that happen to a man? How?”

“Oh leave him be, Rachel. He can’t help it.”

“Can’t he though?”

“I don’t think so. He’s a necessary accoutrement.”

Just then someone tapped me on the shoulder, and I turned.

“So, you going to this?” Colin asked as he waved the sparkling piece of paper in front of me. His eyes were open, his sanguine lips curled up in a smile and I suddenly felt myself blush, and I knew he noticed because the sides of his mouth curled up even more, revealing his perfect, white teeth. I blushed and his perfect teeth told me he liked it.

“I’m sorry?”

“Your friend’s bash. *Cirque Fantastique.*”

"Oh. Well," I said, raising my voice a bit, "Justin's more an acquaintance than a friend."

"You two seemed pretty friendly to me."

"That's just the way Justin is, with everybody."

"I see," he said with a trace of southern drawl. "No crime against being friendly, I suppose."

"Not yet."

"Right," he smiled at me. "Not yet."

"So, are you? Going?" Colin said pointedly after an uncomfortable pause. "I'm only asking, y'know, because I hate to waste my time."

My mouth shut, and my fingers tightened around my drink. I could feel the familiar cold of the ice through the glass as I raised my eyes to meet Colin's. Here was the faun, directly in front of me, a clear shot, his open face before my own, and nothing else mattered. And then I felt a peculiar feeling, one I had never quite felt before. A jolt rippled through my body, from my fingers attached to the glass up through my arm and down the back of my spine. My entire body tingled with anticipation and fear, like one would get by riding a dory into the heart of a storm. I searched the space in front of me for something solid to attach myself to, something to keep me from drowning in the currents overtaking the sinews of my body, and that's when I noticed that Colin had the kind of face that was even more delicate up close. Not many men could say this about themselves, but Colin could. Most men, the closer you get to them the more their features begin to slip out of proportion, pulled out of shape by untamed hairs and awkward lines, but Colin's face kept its grace and symmetry even under close scrutiny. Here was something I could drop anchor into, something that would surely keep me from continuing to drift without a compass.

Just then, Rachel dipped in between us. "Well, then don't bother showing up to anything Justin throws together. He's always a complete waste of time." I had nearly forgotten she was standing right next to me until she spoke and then she giggled, a strange thin sound that stayed above the buzz of music and fading conversations around us. I was suddenly ashamed to be with her.

"Ouch—really? He didn't seem that bad to me, for this town, anyways."

"Justin has his good qualities," I said.

"Sure, somewhere under all the lacquer," Rachel added.

"That does seem to be the way of things around here," Colin said, folding his paper napkin to sit around the top of his beer like a bandana. "I'm not exactly used to all that, yet."

"Trannies?"

"Nah, fictions."

I took the bait willingly. "You haven't been in LA long?"

"Not really, no," Colin replied. "Things are a bit different where I was raised—oh, we have our peculiarities, except where I grew up they were much less tabloid, if y'know what I mean."

"Georgia, or Tennessee?"

"Hey, that's pretty good—I'm a southern transplant, alright, from outside Nashville. Been here nearly two months, now."

"I've been to Nashville—years ago. I can't say that I cared for it, to be honest. A town oversaturated with country music is not exactly my style, except for Dolly of course."

"You been to Dollywood?"

"I haven't actually, but I would."

"Right."

"Don't get me wrong. I do like parts of the South—I moved here from Atlanta myself about a year ago."

"Atlanta, huh. Whereabouts you live?"

"Midtown."

"Hmph," Colin snorted. "Of course."

"Why *of course*?"

"Well, come on. Midtown's the gayest section of Atlanta, see? I mean, you can find everything right under your window box on a breezy day, from books to blow jobs."

"Well, you know us gays. Nothing speaks to us like convenience."

Colin smirked then and relaxed against the railing. He began to play with his napkin again, and that was when I was able to get a long look at his large hands for the first time. They were large and white and very masculine. He wore no rings. Perhaps it was a trick of the light, but his wide, shapely fingernails looked almost pale blue instead of pink, and each was accented with a perfect little crescent of white near the cuticle. None of the white tips of his fingernails showed, and I could see no hair on his fingers. I imagined them on me, touching my back. His large hands were as white as his face, as white and as thick as an Italian statue. They would feel thick on my neck, across my back, between my legs.

"So what brought you to LA, if I may ask?"

"Oh the usual, I suppose."

"Ah. Stardom."

"Movies or modeling, whichever happens first."

"Tough business to crack."

"Well, truth be told, I'm still hard up for work—I know, I know, I shouldn't say something like that here in the middle of West Hollywood."

"You might be transubstantiated into ash," I laughed.

Colin looked at me steadily. I couldn't tell whether he appreciated my joke or if he was annoyed by it, but after a few minutes, he smirked again and continued. "Hmm," he said, "I just told you I'm unemployed, and you're still standing here, and now you're laughing at me."

"Oh, I'm not laughing *at* you, honest."

"Well, then I made you laugh—even better. I guess that means you must like me more than a little."

The music faded into the background, and I began to hear my heartbeat reverberate against the inside of my eardrums. We were a foot away from each other in a manufactured darkness, but I knew that Colin saw the color rise in my cheeks.

Then again, it's possible the first blush never left me.

"Well, I've been out there myself recently," I said.

"Is that right? Cold working the corner of La Cienega and Sunset, isn't it?"

"That's not what I meant," I said, and I locked eyes with him for the first time since our conversation began.

Then the oddest thing happened.

The room pressed in on me, and all the other talk, the background music, the men around me coming and going now dim and stretched far from me, like all of life and living had been sucked through a tube, and I found myself suddenly overlooking the activity below, able only to sense it. There, in that distant place, behind this strange veil that had been pulled in front of me, I witnessed Colin and me. We were moving and talking but I couldn't feel any movement or hear any sound. A glowing border appeared around us, a space between us and everything pressing around us, and we were lit by something beyond my understanding, something powerful and creative. It pulsed white and hot through me, around me, and made itself known to me. It told me that this must be. And then all at once I was back inside my own body, looking out through my own eyes at Colin looking back at me.

"You know," she said, breaking into my conversation with Colin once again, "that extremely chatty neighbor of ours, what's her name?"

Knowing me so well, I'm sure Rachel could tell that I was more than a little interested in Colin, and I found myself actually wishing I had come alone to this place tonight. I didn't want to turn away from Colin to look at Rachel then, not even for a moment, but I had to, otherwise I would've been terribly cruel, and I am not terribly cruel. At least, I never thought of myself as cruel. Still, if the world could have stopped altogether, and Colin and I stayed forever locked in that one moment, secure from anything divine or ill, I would have had it so.

But no perfect moment stays still for long.

I've read books written by prophets who claim we have nothing but our natures to blame for the degradation of all that is good in the world—or we can blame Adam and Eve if we would rather believe that theological nonsense. The truth is, since Eden, all has been just a falling away from one moment to the next to the next until what was once pure and good no longer resembles how it began, until all we have left in our hands are the wafer-round difficulties of regret, hard on the tongue under the thick strike of memory. And memories are often cruel.

"Do you mean Diane?"

"Yes, that one. Isn't she an exec at a temp agency downtown? She can help your new friend here find a job."

"Temp agencies usually deal in secretarial work, though."

Colin shook his head slightly. "You know, at this point, I'd work retail—just as long as it pays the bills. Amazing how those pieces of paper begin to pile up when you ignore them." He then moved his eyes from me to Rachel and back again. "So you two are here together."

"No, well, we came together, if that's what you mean."

"I see," he said knowingly as he leaned back a bit farther against the bar.

"No, you don't understand. Rachel and I moved here together from Atlanta."

Rachel extended her arm in her usual manner, palm down.

"Hi. No misfortune here—I'm a friend."

"Well," Colin said as he reached for Rachel's hand, "I do believe that the misfortune of one is the fortune of another."

"Oh, I like that." Rachel said. "Sounds like a Chinese cookie."

"Nice to meet you, Rachel, even if it is here in this place. My name is Colin." They finished shaking hands, and then he turned his smile on me. "And you?"

"What about me?"

"Do you have a name?"

"Of course I have a name."

"I could guess, but I'd probably be all wrong."

And then Rachel giggled again, a sound that carried itself in the air about us like a hungry mosquito. "Go ahead and guess. What do you think his name is?"

Colin looked at me then in a manner different from how he had been looking at me up until that point, and I felt a rush of excitement laced with impatience and intimidation. For a few moments, I matched his stare, but I was the first to look away, and then down at his hands, which were, in truth, just as unsafe to watch as his eyes.

"Antonio."

"No."

"John-Michael."

"Do I seriously look like a John-Michael?"

"Maybe. You never know in this town."

"You're right there."

"Wait! I know what it is."

"Tell me."

"It's Rumpelstiltskin, right?"

I laughed and looked up again.

"God, I wish. There's nothing but straw in this city. No, it's David – my name is David."

He cocked his head to the side and squinted at me through the flashing of lights and whirling sounds. It was a strange thing to do, I suppose, since we were standing right next to each other. His nose crinkled up a bit, nearly in an expression of distaste, and then the sides of his mouth began to arch themselves into a grin.

"I suppose that name suits you, at least, from what I can see of you in here," he finally said. "I'd have to see you outside in daylight—perhaps with your shirt off—to really be sure."

"My shirt off."

"Come on. Haven't you ever heard of Michelangelo's *David*?"

"Of course—he's in the Piazza della Bella Arte."

"If you say so—I've never been to Italy, but I know he's supposed to be the finest of men, chiseled from the purest of Italian marble, so like I said," Colin paused to sip his beer. "No way for me to tell in here if you're a real David."

"Oh, I'm not perfect."

Colin laughed lightly.

"Really? I didn't think anyone in this place would admit to such a flaw."

At that, Rachel made a face and leaned in towards the two of us. "Look, I'm sure that you two would like to stay here all night and get to know each other better without me hanging around like a bat, so I'm willing to fly off anytime you'd like. The only problem is I didn't drive here."

"So like a woman—Rachel is the one who dragged me out tonight in the first place and now she's the one rushing me home."

"I'm not rushing *you*, David, but I do need to get home," she said firmly. "I don't want to be a spoilsport, really I don't, but it *is* after 1 am and some of us actually want to be on time for work tomorrow."

"You two didn't Uber here?"

"No, I drove, actually," I said. "Took us forever to park."

Rachel put her empty glass down on the space of open bar between Colin and me. Several glasses stood there, not ours, a collection from random people who once stood here, I suppose, or perhaps they were the empty glasses of some of the patrons at another section of the bar that got pushed down towards the sink, placed on hold for washing while the bartender loitered elsewhere.

I raised my eyes and looked at Colin. His face wore a somewhat serious expression as his mind worked to figure out how to best deal with the situation before him.

"Let her have the car," said Colin after a moment. "I'll take you home, later, after we finish talking. Besides, you haven't even offered to buy me a drink."

I stared down at the keys in my hand and saw myself passing them to Rachel as she leaned in close and whispered, "Have a good time—be safe."

"Always," I whispered back.

Colin and I silently watched Rachel make her way through the remaining crowd towards the entrance, and after a quick wave back in our direction, she went through the front door, turned left and began the walk far down Robertson. Once she was gone, Colin and I then moved ourselves further down the bar so that we could be even more alone with one another, but we were quiet for some time until Colin finally spoke.

"I should tell you, if you're looking to get laid tonight, you're chatting up the wrong bird. I'm not easy."

"That's good. I don't like easy."

"Come on, every man likes easy," said Colin with a degree of self-confidence.

"Sure, but not all the time. Where's the fun in that?"

Colin turned away from me and scanned the bar which had by now thinned out considerably. It appeared as if he was looking for something, for someone, as his eyes rested themselves then and again on the few people still around us. I watched him as he searched, and I couldn't help but think to myself that he was being coy. This pretense was meant to throw me off track, surely, but I knew it was just a ruse. He was clearly interested in me.

And the capture of the faun had begun.

"I can use that drink."

"Sure, let's both have another," I replied, even though I had already reached my limit. I began to piece together an excuse for calling into work tomorrow morning. "What are you having?"

"Miller Light. You?"

"Oh," I said, looking at the nearly empty rocks glass in my hand, "I always drink a dirty Kettle over ice, three olives."

"Dirty?"

"Makes it special."

"If you say so. What makes it dirty? Don't tell me the bartender dips his boys in there for you."

"Not without a hefty up-charge. It's olive brine. You can mix brine into gin or vodka, but I only like vodka. The brine provides a thick salty taste, like sea water."

"Sounds nasty."

"It's something you get used to."

At that moment, the bartender who had been flirting with me earlier walked up to our side of the bar and glared at us. "You two ready for another right under last call?"

"Sure, I'm having a Miller Light, and the Captain here is having a dirty Kettle martini."

"Over ice."

"Over ice."

"With three olives."

"With . . ."

"I heard him, thanks." The bartender walked away briskly to dig out the brine from inside a small refrigerator.

"Bartenders in this town are touchy," Colin remarked.

"Touchy feely, usually."

"We got off easy, then."

"But you claim to like easy."

Colin narrowed his eyes and took a good look at me.

"I don't know about you, Michelangelo. I just don't think you're playing the game right."

"I'm not?"

Colin relaxed against the bar with his beer in his right hand and shoved his left hand into his jeans, pulling out a pack of crumpled Marlboro Lights that disappeared quickly back into his pocket, and a collection of bills. He offered me the bills, but I refused them with a wave of my hand.

"No, you're not."

"How am I supposed to play it, then? Tell me."

"A little more mysterious can't hurt. You shouldn't ever give away all your cards even before the deck's shuffled, anyone whose been to Vegas can tell you that. In fact," he said, as he reached across the bar to take another napkin from the holder nearest him, "being transparent in this town is, well, it's sorta taboo, right? Fatal, even."

I can remember that this statement struck me as terrible, dangerous and carnal, but I chose to overlook it at the time. I can remember the heaviness of the men lingering in the space around us. I moved my sight from one man to the next, and it struck me then that all these men, perhaps all the men in West Hollywood, however they were dressed or however they presented themselves, were driven by the same dangerous and carnal forces. All of them, an army of work and play replicas moving in and out of life like shades, getting nowhere except further away from each other across baskets of soiled sheets in between clinic visits. Witnessing so much activity without the promise of completion, at least not completion in any real and meaningful way, left me feeling empty.

"Let's get out of here. No one can have a serious conversation in such a place."

"Sure, where would you like to go?"

"Well, let's down these drinks and then we can go grab some coffee across the street, if you'd like. Or, we can go back to my place. I have an apartment a few blocks from here, a working coffeemaker, and ground coffee from Starbucks that I picked up just this morning."

I smirked at him, then. "I thought you said you weren't easy—already you're asking me over to your apartment?"

"Right. I won't tell mamma if you won't."

* * * * *

Outside, the city was calm and still. For a time, we just stood there, neither one of us willing to take the first step into anything more than passing civility come morning. But somehow we knew it would be much more than that. Somehow we had found each other despite the yards of desperate glances, and the way Colin held my hand there in the calm and still, I was certain that he felt the same way as I did. From that moment on, there would be no one else for me but Colin, and there would be no one else for Colin but me. And this meant that all of it, all of it, was unavoidable from the very beginning, our hands cupped every decision to turn left or right down a street, every decision to sleep in later than usual and every decision to feed the hunger that now coursed through our blood. There may have been something gross working behind our meeting so, but we chose to cast our line of sight only ahead of us and not let anything interrupt our pulse as it beat against each other's wrists.

And then a small crowd of men who took to moving about the night together came towards us, laughing, with their arms lovingly about each other's shoulders. In any other place, such a display would come only from foreigners, Europeans most likely, or other people exempt from the packaging of American behavior. But here in West Hollywood, the scene is cliché, and it presented us with a means to take necessary risk, and so we began to move away from the spot that held us near the doorway for what seemed like an unusually long period of time. We began to walk together, our bodies pressed close enough to make sure no words would be lost or mistaken as we traveled the calm and still.

"Look! Some rats are going home for the night," said Colin pointing out the small crowd ahead of us, "and now the rest of the rats come out." He smiled bleakly and looked to me, and to my surprise, he pulled on my hand to increase our pace. "Come on then, I will show you a small rat apartment that costs far too much money," he said. "You're bound to see it soon enough, anyway."

So I gripped Colin's white thick hand tight and we made our way towards Santa Monica where we would cross and walk steadily onwards for a few blocks until turning left and then right to find ourselves removed from the remaining foot traffic on the nearby boulevard. A streetlamp flickered on the corner, and just as I felt a drop or two of light rain strike my forehead, we turned into the building, climbed up two sets of open cement stairs and stopped just outside Colin's door.

"Well, here we are," he said, as he fumbled with his key in the lock. He tried one key and then another until he found the right one, all the while his hands shook slightly, and I fell deeper in love with him for it. "Don't expect much. I don't have decent furniture yet, and I wasn't expecting company so the place'll be a mess."

"That's okay," I said reassuringly.

The opened door and stale air, heavy and thick with dampness, filled my lungs. Colin didn't immediately switch on a light, but a small table-lamp glowed steadily in the far corner of the room. After a few moments, my eyes adjusted, and I was able to make out an open square room with furniture carefully arranged to give it the appearance of sectioned space. To the right of the front living area, a large bed appeared half-mast behind a standing screen, and a small kitchen was immediately visible on the left, and I could tell that the space was actually a modest studio apartment, with only the bathroom closed off from the rest of the living quarters.

"I'll open the balcony door and a window, for cross ventilation. It gets stuffy in here, not sure why."

As Colin walked through the living area towards a double French door, he bent over a couple of times to pick up random objects left out on the carpet and tossed them into a corner. When the doors to the balcony opened, the cool night air took the heaviness from the room, making the space we were standing in suddenly lighter. Then I noticed that along the side wall were several shelves completely dedicated to books. More books stacked themselves up next to the television, and I went immediately to them.

"Wilde, Forster, Baldwin . . . you certainly have some big guns here."

Colin switched on the overhead in his kitchenette and began brewing the coffee he promised on our walk over here. He measured a few full scoops of grinds, tossed them into the machine, pressed a button and then turned to look at me standing near a stack of his books. Under the pale light of the fluorescent, his eyes stood out, pronounced and saucer-bright, and for a moment I was reminded of the time my parents took me to see Ann Bancroft, Jane Fonda and Meg Tilly in some movie the title of which escapes me. It was about a young woman, played by Tilly, who, isolated in a convent, became impregnated by what she insisted to Mother Bancroft and Detective Fonda, what she insisted was the Divine itself. *Agnes of God* – that's the name of the movie. And Colin, his eyes so large and bright, I saw in them at that moment all the wondrous possibilities of existence, of the way it expands and then curves back into itself with the serenity of a sleeping child. And then I remembered that Agnes, out of innocence or desperation, killed the infant she bore that night, alone in her convent room, and stuffed it into a trashcan.

"I like to read. Some of those books are from college, though. I can't seem to throw any of them away."

"I hate to admit it, but I don't get to read much anymore."

"Sit anywhere you like. The coffee will be ready in a few minutes."

I sat on the part of the sofa closest to where I had been standing and Colin sat right next to me. Our thighs touched through denim, and I couldn't help but imagine what they would look like once he had removed his jeans, once they were bare and wrapped solidly around my own, the fair hair glistening with the light moisture produced from the chafing of bodies, his large white feet, darkened underneath from walking through the dust of the day, banging themselves against the bottom edge of the bed as they were used to find his balance while riding wave after wave on top of and inside my body. And then he laid his large hand on top of mine and chills made their way up my arm and into my neck giving me another sensation of the night ahead of us. For a moment I thought I was going to faint, but then he sat back quickly and put his legs up on the coffee table which was littered with newspapers and used glasses. His sudden movement steered my attention away from the pictures still playing inside my mind.

"You don't like to read?"

"Oh, I like to read, but I don't get to do it for pleasure too often. Between prepping for classes and grading student papers, I don't have the time for reading like I used to. I miss it."

"That's too bad," Colin said thoughtfully. "I couldn't live without books. Some people feel that way about music, which I also like a sure lot, some people feel that way about Netflix, God help them. I feel that way about books. I can't get enough of them, and I keep buying more."

"Ah, you're the one."

"Right—you found me."

"Quite an oddity in this town."

"I suppose that's right, isn't it. Sad, really, when you think about it."

"What kind of books do you like most?"

"Don't judge me, but right now, I'm into fantasy." He crossed his legs and then added, "And philosophy." Colin ran his fingers through his curly blonde hair, pulling some of it forward across his forehead. "My favorite author of late is H.G.Wells."

"I do like philosophy—but that's quite different from fantasy, isn't it?"

Colin cocked his head to the side and squinted at me for a second. "Well," he started, "that depends on what kind of fantasy you're reading, and what kind of philosophy you're used to living, I suppose."

I looked at him expectantly.

"Take Ursula LeGuin, for instance," Colin continued as he got up and went over to the bookshelves. "Granted it's a bit sophomoric, but the *Earthsea* series is really a detailed description of a life philosophy, and her best work."

"Better than *The Dispossessed*?"

"Oh, yes, I think so. *Earthsea* requires that we face our demons, however scary or dangerous, and that we exercise great will in making sure they submit to the higher part of our consciousness. It's a philosophy based on action, not only thought. I suppose that's why I like it so much. Thought without action is sort of cowardly, don't you think?" He squatted and pulled at a few books on the second to bottom shelf until they came loose, and then he carried them back to where we had been sitting. "Here."

"*Wizard of Earthsea*, *The Tombs of Atuan*, *The Farthest Shore*."

"There was a fourth and final book in the series. Came out many years later, called *Tuhuna*, or something like that, but I didn't want to buy it."

"*Tehanu*," I corrected.

"That's it," he said. "I thought you didn't like fantasy?"

"I didn't say that, exactly. I said I liked philosophy—I've read this series before, and I remember enjoying it immensely when I was young."

"Young, right," he said with chastisement. "You make it sound as if you're a Redwood. I see this city's already gotten to you." The coffee maker let off a high tone, indicating that it was finished brewing, and Colin jumped up towards the kitchen once again. "You're not old, David."

"No, perhaps not, but I am older than you."

"Is that a problem?"

"Not with me."

"Then why bring it up?"

"I guess I want to know how you feel about it."

"If it mattered to me, you wouldn't be in my apartment in the middle of the night," he replied as he began pouring coffee into two matching blue mugs that he had removed from the dishwasher. "Sugar, milk?"

"Four sugars, no milk."

"*Four* sugars?"

"I like my coffee sweet and dark, always have."

"It's your diabetic coma," he said as he put one spoon of sugar after another into my cup.

"So why didn't you buy the last book in the series?"

Colin began to move back to our space on the sofa. "I couldn't bring myself to read it I suppose." He continued as he set the mugs he was carrying down. "The first three books are a near perfect blend of fantasy and philosophy. I didn't want anything to disturb that."

"Only near perfect?" I asked.

"Well," Colin said, fingering one of his curls, "*nothing* is perfect, right?"

A silence lingered in the air while Colin and I sipped on our coffee. Colin was looking away from me, out into the open space before us, and it gave me time to study his profile. His nose turned up slightly at the tip, and his chin stuck out passed his bottom lip like it should.

"This evening is turning out to be far better than I expected," I said finally.

"You don't have to say that."

"No, I mean it, Colin. You're the first guy I've met in West Hollywood I'd actually like to see again."

"That's because I don't *come* from here," Colin was quick to remind me. "Nashville is the other side of the world. Here in LA, there are these rules of behavior that I just don't get, and I certainly don't appreciate. Everything in me, my upbringing, my beliefs, my thought processes, even the way I walk, seems to be in direct violation of some code of conduct that West Hollywood forces onto the people who live here. In Nashville, I sang in a choir and went to the gym only when I felt like it. Here, everyone hires a trainer and goes to the gym as many times a week as they can—and no one attractive sings in a choir. I've been here for three months, right, and in all that time I haven't been able to connect with anyone, really connect with anyone, because all the people I meet in bars and clubs, especially the ones off Tinder, are so shallow a tadpole couldn't survive inside them for a day without suffocating" Colin paused and reached for my hand again. "But you seem to be different."

"That's because I don't come from LA, either."

Colin laughed his fountain laugh and leaned his head into my chest.

THREE

For the next six weeks, I practically quit my apartment with Rachel and attached myself to Colin inside his studio off Santa Monica. I saw Colin every day and slept next to him every night, and I admit freely that this time was the best time of my life. Nothing else seemed to matter, either. It didn't matter that the room remained stuffy during the day until we threw the balcony doors open. It didn't matter that we liked our coffee brewed at different strengths—we simply made two pots in the morning, and he always let me brew mine first. It didn't matter that the space we found ourselves in was so tight a bird would shit on itself if it had been caged with us. The close quarters only seemed to increase our desire to be with each other and it often spilled into quick and fevered lovemaking across every square foot of the small space. Essays that needed grading began to pile up in a spot on his coffee table, phone calls from friends back east didn't get returned. I even stopped seeing Rachel with any urgency. Life with Colin became an all-consuming occupation, one that demanded only that it be responsible to itself. With singular priority it squeezed out all other considerations and fed on every part of me like a fetus inside a womb. It eclipsed my desire to live singularly and alone, and before I knew it, I could find myself only with difficulty.

During this span of time together, despite the way in which our lives flowed as twin currents that slipped on top of one another, Colin became more and more frustrated when it came to expenses. He had been trying nearly every day but still hadn't been able to find a job aside from occasionally temping for some downtown agency, and his savings were running dangerously low. This gnawed at him constantly, and it began to affect the atmosphere around us, draining it of color. As much as we were intoxicated with each other, our drunkenness couldn't dilute Colin's feeling inadequate somehow. I told him not to worry about it, that money would take care of itself and that we should enjoy our time together in our square of space before circumstances forced our situation to change, but that seemed to just make matters worse. He told me once that telling him not to worry about money made him feel like an old dog getting patted on its head before being led outside to be shot dead. I didn't care too much for the metaphor, but I understood what he meant by it.

I tried to soothe him whenever possible, but the truth is, I understood Colin's frustration. It's hard to feed any creative desire, any passion, without first meeting the basic requirements of life. In a way, I suppose this is the cruel irony of art itself—it grows only in a seeded environment, and this means someone must first labor to plant and then continue to tend the seeds. Without this mundane toil, without the basics of hard and repeated work, there could be no foundation on which to create something beautiful, to create art. And the love Colin and I grew together in our West Hollywood cocoon surely was art if it was anything.

Colin understood this—perhaps better than I did—which is why he insisted on tilling his own earth.

Early one Saturday, still in my morning robe, I finished my second cup of rich coffee and went towards the balcony to smoke a cigarette and sit in one of the two large, matching red Adirondack chairs we kept out there for quiet times. When Colin emerged from around the screened off bedroom area, he was fully dressed. He made his way out to the balcony, plopped himself in the chair next to me, and announced that he was, that very day, determined to get a job and end his dependence on my wallet. I insisted once again that I did not care about money. That I have never truly cared about money. I told him that he was welcome to take his time to chart his course, to spend his afternoons with me right here on this balcony in the pursuit of reading or writing, should he feel the urge to write, or even to go back to college and finish his baccalaureate, but he made his face take on the familiar frown and looked from where we were sitting out over the balcony and into the garden area below.

A wind rustled, and as leaves parted in the branches of the large maple that grew in the center of the open space before us, sunlight moved in scattered radiance across his face.

"Oh, you just refuse to understand," he protested at first mildly, clasping his hands behind his large head and leaning a bit back, his eyes still resting themselves on the collection of flora in front of us. "I can't continue to live this way, David, as much as I love you. Actually, it's because I *do* love you so much that I can't continue to be such a burden."

"Don't be ridiculous, Colin—you are not a burden."

Colin removed his hands from behind his head, scrunched his lower lip up under his front teeth and crossed his arms in front of him. He let out a long, low sigh, and after a brief time, he began again in a deliberate tone. "I'm not being ridiculous, David."

"Well I think you are."

At that Colin moved his large white hands onto the arms of his chair with an audible clap that startled me. "Take these chairs, for instance."

"I thought you liked them?"

"I do like them, yes, but, well, here they are on my balcony, and yet, who bought them? You bought them."

"So what? I bought them because I thought it would be nice for us to have some place to sit out here quietly together. I get as much out of them as you do."

Colin sighed again, and I could tell that he was trying his best to let go of some of the irritation he was obviously feeling over our conversation. When he began to speak again, it was even more slowly. "Right. You're right of course. It is nice to have a place to sit out here together, especially when the weather is like this," he admitted while edging a bit towards me. Colin paused again for a moment, cast his eyes downwards at his hands, which were now folded neatly in his lap, took a deep breath and continued. "But try to understand what I am saying here. I know you bought these chairs for us, that you bought them out of kindness, David, but they were expensive—"

"Not really."

"—and all it does is highlight for me the fact that I couldn't afford to buy them *for myself.* Each time we sit out here, each time I come out here, I am reminded of that fact, and it irks me to no end—as much as I appreciate having them in the first place, I'm irked by their very presence. Can't you understand that? The same thing goes with our new coffee maker. There was really nothing wrong with the old one, but you wanted a new one—"

"I wanted a *better* one," I corrected.

"That's exactly what I mean! The one I had was perfectly fine."

"Not really, Colin. It didn't make coffee strong enough for me. There's nothing I dislike more than brown water in the morning."

Colin crossed his arms again and breathed slowly out through his nose. "Well it made coffee strong enough for *me*. But *you* wanted a new coffee maker—no, a *better* one—and so you go and buy one. You bought a new comforter for the bed because the old one wasn't soft enough, new pillows for the sofa because the ones I had didn't go with the color on the walls apparently—hell, last week you would've purchased an entirely new dining set if I didn't absolutely insist against it."

While Colin continued to complain in this way, I couldn't help but feel a bit under-appreciated. The chairs, the pillows, the comforter—even the coffee maker, despite Colin's tolerance of the old one—all of these items were purchased to make our life together better. I bought them to improve our space not complicate it or bring out this resentment in Colin which, frankly, surprised me. I suppose that when he first started talking to me about his concerns that morning, I didn't really want to hear what Colin was saying to me. The negative energy beginning to edge into our sanctuary was just too foreign to land well. But as we continued to sit there together, once Colin had finished his little diatribe, I took the time to review in my mind what he had just finished saying to me, and I tried really hard to understand where Colin was coming from, and soon I began to make sense of his words in a way that I could comprehend. Perhaps he was truly ashamed by the improvements I made to the studio. Perhaps he was feeling that I was replacing objects in the apartment, piece by piece, and erasing his sense of ownership along with it. Perhaps he was just being stubborn—or playfully combative. Whatever the cause, he was clearly unhappy with the fact that he had no purchasing power of his own, no agency, perhaps even in our relationship, and I began to see how that made him into a person unsettled and restless.

"We bought all of those things together," I said quietly.

At that, Colin narrowed his eyes and pushed forward with the crux of his argument. "Well, sure, I was *there* when *you* purchased them, yes, but I didn't lay out any money—not for any of it."

"I didn't realize that all of this bothered you that much."

"Bother me? No," he lifted his arms up and cradled my face with his large masculine hands. He cradled my face with his large hands whenever he wanted to really get me to understand him, to hear him, and most of the time it worked. "Heck, nothing you do truly *bothers* me, David. But I do feel more than a little guilty living off your fat paychecks like this," he said with another audible sigh. "Don't misunderstand me. I'm grateful you're such a generous person, I love you all the more for it, but this is still my apartment technically and I should be the one to furnish it—or at least contribute to its being furnished," he paused for a moment and then ended with a flourish of his arms as he collapsed back into his chair, "Heck, it's like I'm a kept man!"

I closed my eyes and my mouth and sat there in silence for a minute. I let his last words wash over me, through me—*a kept man?* How silly a concept, truly. This was so far from what I believed to be true, what Colin knew to be true, that I was more than willing to just shrug it off as the kind of conjecture one makes in the heat of a moment. There simply could be no truth in such a conclusion, for it would mean that Colin could indeed *be* kept—an impossible notion that would mean Colin was little more than a glorified whore, and I'd be damned if I let myself believe he could be something as common as that. Worse, if Colin were a kept man, then that would mean that I was his keeper, and that was not the kind of relationship either of us wanted because there were no guarantees in a conditional, replaceable agreement. The idea struck me as completely indecent, and I am sure my face showed just how uncomfortable I had become because Colin reached out and took my hand tenderly in his.

"And besides, I need my independence back. I want to be able to buy us dinner every once in a while, and I need some new clothes—and I need to do something with my time other than sit around here most of the day and look pretty for you—otherwise I won't be happy in this arrangement for too much longer. And I want to be happy with you, forever, isn't that what you want? For me to be happy with you forever?"

"It's what I intend," I answered.

"Then," he said softly as he stood up and put his arms around my shoulders from behind and, kissing me lightly on the top of my head, insisted, "tell me 'Good luck!' and nothing more."

I should have said something else to him; I should have set some limit or definition to his pursuit—something that would have offered him some lines inside which he could draw, could color wildly if he must. Safe margins. But I knew there was little point in arguing over circumstances such as these. After everything that he expressed to me that morning on the balcony, it was clear that Colin needed to feel he was contributing to our life together, and to feel a sense of purpose beyond, well, me, and so I said the only thing left for me to say.

"Good luck!"

I said good luck because it was the only thing that Colin left me to say.

* * * * *

After Colin left, I remained outside for some time. I found the space pleasant and distracting since the view from our balcony offered a lot to fill the senses. It jutted out into a central courtyard-like area lined with other balconies overhanging first floor patios. Peering over the side I could see thin sidewalks joining the patios below to a circular pathway inside which grew an elaborate collection of exotic flora. The summer sun sent its heat down into the center of the space and pulled every bud open, revealing bromeliad, white jasmine, pink hibiscus and climaxing into the delicate folds of Angel's Trumpet. In the middle of all of these white and pink hues grew a magnificent and aged flowering maple in full bloom. Its branches and leaves crisscrossed the sunlight, breaking it into patches of light and shade over much of the surrounding area, and its blossoms filled the air with a faint floral scent. I could tell by the size of its trunk the tree must've been standing there for some time, its roots digging deeply into the soil around it in all directions. It was a garden now grown wild within the limits of its space, but it was clear to me that someone once paid a good deal of attention to it, nonetheless.

Two people, a man and a woman in their thirties, moved outside on a patio across from where I stood. I didn't want to pry, but their harried and raw appearance begged my attention, and I casually stood up and leaned into the side of the building to mask most of my frame so I could watch without being seen. I watched as these two people became more and less animated during their conversation, and even though I was too far away from them to overhear their words, I could tell from their gestures and positions that they broached subjects uncomfortable. All at once, he shot forth a hand and pointed it at her, and that was when she turned away from him; after a short time, he walked over to her and placed his other hand atop her shoulder in a delicate fashion. At his touch, she spun around to regard him once more. Then she moved out from him and pulled herself to the other side of the cement square, and, facing him once again, began to gesticulate at him under the sun-drenched sky. He stood still during this latest barrage. He appeared to be listening to her until her words stopped their assault, then he crossed his arms and shook his head in some display of disbelief or refusal. They stayed on opposite sides of the space for a short time, and then, as if by compulsion, the couple moved closer together, and, finally, he placed his arms around her waist, and they shared the kind of embrace that carried weight.

They went through the open sliding glass door and disappeared into what I assumed to be the apartment they shared across from the one I shared with Colin.

I let my mind run over what I had witnessed. First I imagined a rather cliché situation had unfolded before me: she found out that she was pregnant, a surprise to both of them since she had been on the pill for months, and now they were locked into either aborting the child or getting married; after a heated discussion that included accusation and the quick assignment of blame, they decided in the end to get married. Then I thought: perhaps the two were sister and brother, and they were arguing over who should be the executor of their recently departed mother's estate; after each sibling put the other's selfish motives on notice, they decided what their mother would've wanted was for them to share the burden equally. Another possibility: she caught him in a lie, a terrible lie, and he couldn't believe that he had been so careless, so reckless in fact, as to allow himself to be caught in that lie—now, with the lie opened in sunlight, with the truth revealed in that no-longer gray space, they would have to deal with the lie turned truth as both would come to know it.

Sometime later, Colin returned to find me still on the balcony. After allowing my mind to wander for a time about the couple across the way, I must've crawled into one of the Adirondack chairs and fallen asleep there. He took the other chair, leaned back into it and nudged me with the toe of his shoe until I came around. When I fully opened my eyes, I saw displayed a broad smile on his face. I could tell right away that his mission had been successful.

"Well, you are looking at the brand-new bartender at *Ici*," he said with tangible pleasure.

"Sure, right."

"No I mean it—I start this weekend."

"You're serious. Do you even know how to bartend?"

"Not really, no. But I'm a quick study. One of the bar managers, Francois, was there. He took one look at me and practically hired me on the spot."

"So he hired you on your looks alone, eh? I know a number of dirty names for people like you."

Colin tilted his head back away from me and forced a bit of his fountain of a laugh and then said, "Well, he had me bang out a few keys on the register, pour a beer out of a tap and then badly make a Cosmopolitan. I mean, it was nowhere near pink. Then he hired me. I'm working this Friday, evening shift."

"Wow. Weekend shifts right out the gate—unusual, but impressive I suppose."

Colin sighed and folded his hands behind his head. He closed his eyes and turned his face towards the sun that was still filtering down onto the balcony where we both sat in wooden chairs facing the tropical garden. His grin remained.

"I knew that being pretty would pay off in this town eventually—it was just a matter of time."

For some reason, these words seemed dangerous to me. I imagined him tooling in the space behind the bar, searching for the correct bottle among many, fumbling his way through a variety of poorly made cocktails to appease the black little eyes, only to have them squint queerly at him across the top of a straw. I saw him struggling to measure the proportions of a Long Island Iced Tea or bungling through one blended mistake after another without worrying about the security of his position because his majestic face, tall stature and solid build would prevent him from being called out for bad service. And then there was the entire matter regarding how he would get paid for working in such an establishment. Bartenders in LA, especially those in cruisy West Hollywood clubs, are expected to work for their tips, and that means maintaining a certain *joie de vivre*—which includes wearing tight-fitting jeans, going shirtless in the well, playing games of winks and blushes, and making sure that they always look like they've stepped off an Abercrombie and Fitch photo shoot—all to lure in yet another widely circulated dollar from yet another drunk, fondle-happy queen.

Nevertheless, I did my best to keep my doubts to myself as we sat out on the balcony for some time longer, absorbing the quiet of the evening. I suppose I could have taken that opportunity to tell Colin about the couple and the heated discussion I witnessed, but I didn't. I decided that I really couldn't tell him about what I didn't know, and that speculation about the couple's predicament wouldn't be fair to either the couple or to Colin.

Besides, there was no need to make Colin suspicious of people around him or to spread rumors, and so we sat quietly facing the garden and let the now fading summer heat play itself along our skin, and soon the couple and their danger faded into the cold recess of memory.

* * * * *

It is memory that haunts me now, here on the Mediterranean, where it does not often grow cold. Currents stay warm and full of electricity off the North African shore. But for the past half hour the temperature has been falling rapidly and the wind has picked up some, perhaps due to the increased speed of the vessel that carries me. To be honest, the entire trip has been without the usual warmth of the season, though the people on board who spent good sums of money to escape near-winter chill seem to take it as ill-breeding in a fellow traveler if he makes any reference to this fact. Even when the coarse wind and salt stings their faces and eyes, the wind and salt penetrate everything, even then travelers pass each other on deck and smile as radiantly as children with the expectation that the sun will be out and overhead again later that afternoon and, if not then, certainly by tomorrow. Yes, certainly by tomorrow.

I quit the balcony and the railing outside and re-enter the small floating apartment, and something in me decides that it would be best to leave this cabin for a while, negotiate my way through some sort of buffet and eat again before the night becomes blacker and more hostile—I decide to shave first—but before I can make my way to stand before the mirror in the small washroom I hear a knock on the door. Some part of me enlivens from the prospect of a distraction from my brooding thoughts, but then I hear a female voice come from the hall, a high-whining and rather persistent voice, *Monsieur Russo! Monsieur Russo are you in there!* My desire for distraction now gone from me, I wonder, somewhat annoyed, why on earth the girl should be at my door so worried and so insistent.

But she smiles at once when I swing open the cabin door, the kind of smile which immediately tells me that she has been standing somewhere recently with a cocktail in her hand. She is quite thin and not really all that pretty, but pleasant enough to look at while speaking to her, I suppose. Like most of the other young, single women on board the ship, she'd been transported from a state of depression and isolation on shore to a near-feverish mood manufactured on the sensual expectancy of sea travel, as if the ship itself brings with it touch and human warmth. And then I recognize her as the young woman who sits across from me on the round part of our assigned table in the main dining room. Her dress grips her hips tightly, her breasts nearly push themselves up to her chin, and I realize that she is perhaps not so young as I had first thought. I look at her in silence for a moment and begin to create an elaborate backstory for her sudden appearance. Images, some fresh and some sour, take shape, forming and un-forming themselves in my mind, but something in me stopped myself from making up yet another story. I decide instead to see her for what she is, a woman without a proper chaperone, and I am content to leave the cause for her sudden appearance at that.

"Monsieur Russo—I hope you have not locked yourself in your cabin because you are feeling ill?"

"No," I say, "I am not sick."

The woman comes in, letting the door close with a slight slam behind her that startles her some and makes her left hand pop onto her breasts. "*Sacré-Coeur!*"

"Wind—it's blowing outside."

"*Sans blague,* yes!" she says. "It is horrible. Up on deck, no direction is safe. It is obvious why you have hidden yourself in here then."

I say nothing as I set the glass on the armrest of the nearest chair.

"So, Monsieur Russo, we missed you at dinner tonight—I hope it is okay that I have come to talk to you in your cabin. I do not mind if you drink," she said as she pointed to the glass on the chair nearest her, "but you must eat, too, *non*? We cannot have you facing this wind and go up and down the decks of this wonderful ship with hunger, you know."

Her eyes search my face for permission to enter further into the cabin and perhaps to sit, and I stand aside slightly to let her pass fully into the space and take a seat on the chair next to the arm that holds my melting ice in a glass with the vodka she pointed out for me.

"Monsieur Rus—"

"Please, call me David," I say as I raise my hand.

That gets a slight blush from her.

"Ah, *Daa*-vid. Very good. *Et moi*," she says indicating herself, "*je m'appelle Caterine*."

"*Enchanté*"

"Oh but Monsieur *Daa*-vid has not told me *qu'il parle français*."

It is now my turn to blush as Catherine leans in towards me, and all I have to give her engorged bosom are simple words. I have nothing else for her.

"I know very little French, though, *un peu*."

"*Un peu*. This is well. You need to know only a little French today, the language is not as it used to be. Oh well. Of course, neither is France. God bless our country but she has become, *comment dire,* like a whore in the world, *n'est-ce pas*? Packing and unpacking herself as the winds blow. No more *la vie des innocentes*," but her eyes then move slightly to focus behind me, and that's when she sees my suitcase open on the bed with some of my clothes arranged neatly inside. "We are away three days—do not tell me that you have not unpacked?"

"No, well, I may be leaving in the morning," I say, and then I quickly add, "I have business back in the States that demands my return."

"*Vraiment? C'est dommage*, *Daa*-vid. And what is this busy-ness that it takes you from such a beautiful place in the middle of the sea?"

"It can't be helped, I'm afraid."

"*Bien trop tôt alors*, how terribly sad—we will be sorry to see you go—and just when we were all getting to be friends. I hope it is not something too serious?"

"No," I say, "Not too serious."

I am embarrassed and resentful immediately after dismissing Colin and all that he had meant to me as something not too serious. That I should have to do so to quell the curiosity of the insipid Catherine before me only makes the entire sensation worse and more threatening. If I had a knife in my hand, I would plunge it into her to stop her mouth, I would, but I am afraid of her eyes, and I am beginning to sweat. It strikes me then that this young woman, with her dark hair and eyes, reminds me of Rachel, so I turn around and face away. I don't want to see in Catherine's eyes what Rachel saw if she found Colin dead that morning. And something more—I begin to feel the stone weight of public inquisitiveness, its siege of my privacy. It wants my heart—for wouldn't all of Los Angeles and, yes, perhaps the entire world, need to know how and why Colin died? How and why, how and why, with penetrating conjecture over and over. And what if I cut out my heart and give it to them, and tell the how and the why—once Rachel knows the how and why, would I then be forgiven?

"I do not believe you, of course," she says as she touches my chin tenderly to turn my face towards hers, "I can see in your eyes that whatever this busy-ness is must be serious. Still, I hope it is not too hard, whatever it is you must do?"

I don't know how to answer her question. Catherine must see this in my expression, no doubt, for she raises her hands suddenly as if in supplication, stands and crosses to open the cabin door, and makes to leave me with my unspoken thoughts. In the threshold, she pauses, and turns back to me briefly, "Just one thing more, if you will let me say it. Don't live always so serious, *Daa-vid* Russo. It isn't good for a soul to be miserable all the time. *Au revoir, mon ami.*"

As soon as she departs, I would have given anything for her to remain a bit longer. It happens to me, now and then, that people come into my space abruptly, bringing resentment, only to depart too quickly for me to reconcile their leaving. In and out, like a whore unpacking herself in the wind. As it is, with Catherine now gone, I am left to face myself once again in the mirror, razor in hand, but instead of beginning to lather, I put down the blade and turn my eyes away from my reflection and try to force them inward, but I see there only shadows and shadows of shadows, and there is not yet any clear image of what I should do to face the truth welling up inside me.

The hunger now gone, I sit on the bed to wait for daybreak when the winds will surely die down and I will be compelled to enter a new day. I sleep a few hours I suppose, and my dreams begin to whisper themselves into existence as I lay there seduced by the silence of time traversing wave after wave of the sea.

PART TWO

ONE

Between Colin and me, time passed strangely and remotely in the studio apartment just off the boulevard in West Hollywood. At first, there seemed to be no pace, no movement at all, the hours sat still with us, stuck as we were in the joy of finding one another despite the circus just outside our door. The chance of meeting someone like me in a world nearly devoid of sweetness and light had been so remote to Colin, and he told me often that he was very lucky to have me in his life, and I believed him. We considered ourselves to be extremely lucky, and we took great pains to share that notion with one another.

Often, Colin would hide little endearing notes for me in the pockets of my jeans or tape them inside a textbook I was currently using in my classes. In his fanciful cursive, these notes sometimes consisted of just our initials drawn inside a heart in red marker; other times, they contained deliberate phrases that he would write out to capture his affection, simple phrases like "My life began the day we met" and "Think of me today and smile." It is one thing to say such things aloud; it is quite another to put them on paper, able to be referenced. These notes proved that I had captured the faun, and the conquest made me content with life again.

Colin demonstrated his love for me in other endearing ways, too. There was his insistence that we eat dinner together whenever our schedules allowed it. At first, I didn't know how well this house rule of his would work out, exactly, with my classes sometimes running late and with his bar shifts often starting before regular dinner hours, but he made our time together pass well whenever he could. On the evenings when Colin was not working, I enjoyed elaborate dinners consisting of several courses intensified by delicate sauces that took hours of seasoned care to prepare just right—a masterpiece of culinary effort. And then there was the routine attention that he paid to our surroundings soon after I once pointed out to him the studio's state of disarray. From that day forward, he started to spend a lot of energy every week cleaning our small space to ensure that all surfaces sparkled free of dust and that every item, his and mine, were in their proper places—this provided us with a good amount of consistency, and it showed me that he truly cared about my opinion when it came to our living space. And then there was his continued dedication to maintaining our collective routine; every Saturday morning, he would accompany me to the gym to suffer tedious aerobic exercise together, even when he came home after two in the morning from bartending the night before. Yes, Colin made life with him enjoyable in every way, and that's why I believed him when he told me that he was lucky to have me in his life.

In turn, I would never take my eyes off him, having never lost the notion that happiness can escape when it goes unnoticed, and I would bring him bouquets of fresh dahlias—blue and white bursts that filled the studio with fragrant symmetry—from the little stand that stood against the corner of our street. I'd make sure to share with him the events of my day, even when they were dull or without distinction, and then we would spend all evening in some process of lovemaking that climaxed each night in the familiar warmth and comfort of our oversized bed.

From the outside, our relationship must have seemed sickly sweet, like a piece of overripe fruit hung low from heat, but we cared nothing about all that; we deliberately shut ourselves inside our nutshell of space, letting no one and nothing in, besides Rachel who visited every now and then. Even when we opened the door to her, and Rachel sat just there or stood just there, while she would tell us insipid details about her work week or while she would share with us her latest hopeful expectations about some rough guy she recently met in a bar, we would smile and nod and engage her in friendly conversation, but between Colin and me there ran an undercurrent at once transcendent and wordless. Even when we engaged Rachel in friendly conversation, Colin and I were as two starfish entangled at the bottom of the ocean floor, united and silent. Yes, we knew how lucky we were to live so remotely, and I found myself thinking little of Gabriel, if at all. I tried not to think of him at all. If under our great joy there lingered an anguish and a fear that my past would rise like a terrible fish and insist to make itself known to me, to us, at some future moment, I did not let myself doubt for even a second just how lucky I was to once again dwell in an ocean.

But then something strange began to occur, something I have a hard time explaining to myself because I have a logical mind. I am sure I have a logical mind. Despite the undercurrent, or maybe because of it, we were no longer able to keep time with us.

Time began to move with unexpected symphony, slowing and quickening, slowing again and quickening again, depending on how we played the hours. If we sat still with each other, our conversations would fill the urgency of an allegro, and if we lay on top of each other, each down-stroke would hold our flesh in a sustained adagio. At first the change in pace back and forth seemed to not affect us at all. Somehow, as if by magic, our undercurrent rose above the shifting pace, a deliberate tone, vast in frequency. I know it. It was a kind of paradox, surely, to be at once suspended in time and subject to its determining force, but in the mornings we shared and especially at night, all we would hear was our own comfortable key with measured clarity. At these times I would see the glow form in and around us, a whiteness of will that scaled all potential cacophony. It was a reticence supernatural perhaps, otherworldly even.

Before too long, though, we began to force the world itself to match our frequency. If chance found us holding hands along the boulevard, everyone and everything that crossed our line of sight glistened in a haze of promise, and even the sun seemed to be a little higher each morning we took to walking together, hands clasped. Local shop windows glistened with a comforting stillness even well into the night and bars spilling drunken patrons spilling into the street radiated a dynamic energy that pulsed just under our touch. Aside from when Colin was working, we rarely entered any of the bars, but when we did it was with singular purpose—to celebrate our having found one another in a world so misdirected and lonesome. If chance found us stepping inside one of the bars along Santa Monica to drink to our exhilarated spirits, it didn't take long before we'd part the dismal sea of those collected there with clasped hands and a grin. It exalted us.

In such a state, a nearly entranced state, routine became fantastic. I would marvel at how the morning paper would arrive always at six-thirty, its thud against the apartment door would wake me with a now accustomed jolt. I would marvel at how I would then remove myself delicately from under the curve of Colin's arm to brew dark coffee and smoke a cigarette on the balcony and read in the paper about the miseries of the world erupting far from our perfect acre. I would marvel at how the Iraqi war continued to press and to burn despite the last election, at how children secreted semi-automatics into schools to catch America off guard again and again, at how disease and famine and poverty strangled tight the entire African continent, at how the housing market rose only to fall into despair and ruin leaving destitute people impotent and angry—my poor Good Anna!—it was a slow moving apocalypse each morning that bewildered me. There was always something grossly disturbing in the paper, and I would marvel at it all, but I would marvel most at how the cumbrance of the world never came further into our space than the morning. The glow Colin and I shared, it held the intricacies of the universe itself, its desperation and discord, at far distance, and there was something powerfully creative about that glow.

Often, Colin would sleep in until he heard me come out of the shower and begin to dress. Then he would leap out of bed, part the curtains in the living area to let in the morning sunlight and then insist to hold me close to him for a time before allowing me leave for campus. Sometimes, as we curled up on the sofa in this morning repose, he would chat about catches of dreams he remembered from the night before. His dreams were always mundane in scope—walks along an unmanned beach or drives to nowhere in particular; short scenes devouring food at unknown, unnamed restaurants—but they nevertheless presented themselves as twisted and odd, full of motley color and light that ran together confused and larger than life; at times his dreams made us laugh for there was nothing for us to do but laugh at the way in which the ordinary had been transposed into the far-fetched or even the absurd, a definite consequence of our being so sure of ourselves. At other times, he would talk to me at length about some book he was reading in order to invite me into a compelling plot-twist and experience it with him.

It's strange, because I am a teacher of literature, but I can't name any of those books now, their titles somehow lost to me—I must have put their names out of my mind. But I remember some of the plots. I can even hear Colin's voice in my head telling me about them: there was the one about a philosopher, a master game player, and he was embroiled in a stalemate debate over the purpose of art in society; there was the one about an uncomfortable spy turned double-agent who found himself in prison confessing a thin innocence before his execution the following morning; and there was the one about a desperate and troubled man who escapes a life of known misery only to find himself trapped by circumstances in an even larger misery. I would listen earnestly to Colin talk to me about these books, these title-less books, and so many more, but here in the gray and hazy space of time that exists between day and night in which I lay out-stretched across the bed in my stateroom, I can remember only the plots of these three.

And we passed like this, at times quickened and at times slowed, but always suspended in the sanctified space we forged around us, we scarcely felt the passing of seasons. Each day was the same as the one before it, and each day was new. And with each new day came the pleasure of seeing each other work in and through each other's life with the promise of silkworms. We rose together and ate together and walked together and read together. We kept pace with one another, rose and ate and walked and read. And the pace stretched itself out before us, day after day, week after week, month after month, until we barely could tell the passing of seasons.

* * * * *

We didn't really want to step outside the studio together that entire summer, we had nested there so, but on late afternoons when we had an overwhelming desire to be seen and admired as a couple, Colin and I would take a deliberate stroll through the neighborhood to catch glimpses of ourselves reflected in the shop and bar windows that lined the active thoroughfare of West Hollywood. With the sun low sending patterns of light across the bluest of skies, we would give in to our compulsion and walk the entire length of the gay space, stopping here and there to bend into a conversation about whatever grand or small plans we set for ourselves now that life had brought us together.

During one exceptionally public walk, we dropped our pace after passing an outdoor rack brimming with fliers and zines that spoke with urgency on a wide array of contemporary topics, from the true and unbelievable story behind Obamacare to the seductive call of a gay cruise line, and we fell to talking about going on a vacation soon to some faraway and mystical place like Bali or Belize, but after some fanciful discussion we settled on the shores of South Beach since Colin had let his passport lapse last year without renewal and this meant that there would be no leaving domestic territory. And since neither one of us had ever been to Florida (I tried to go once with Samuel many years ago, but the trip never materialized), we decided rather excitedly that the sun under a new angle with an excursion to the Keys would be exotic enough and foreign enough for us to explore together with sincere interest—it was that very trip that produced the photo we cherished so much that we kept it out in full view so that anyone who entered our apartment would bear witness to our framed happiness, and it is that same photo that now sits, with twin smiles oppressive, on the nightstand inside the cabin I occupy so far from where we shared that happiness so easily.

Now that I think about it, Colin and I made a number of serious decisions on our occasional movements up and down the

West Hollywood façade. On another such late afternoon walk through the neighborhood, we spent some words discussing the studio and its tight space and whether we should quit it for larger accommodations, but then a man moved passed us alone with a look on his face we no longer recognized, and we wrapped ourselves around each other like twin vines overtaking a trestle and continued to move along the pavement renewed in our determination to hold fast to our small isolation with its view of the lush inner garden and its careful and sustainable promise. The truth was, we needed no more soil or light to grow our love beyond that room and balcony; the measured space fed us, it sustained us and our love all summer—why mess with something so precise and sure?

But most of the time, if I just wanted to stretch my legs and walk the neighborhood for a bit of exercise, I would venture out alone—especially on Sunday mornings. Then, I would leave Colin early just after breakfast, his eyes fixed on the newspaper, and I would take a walk along the boulevard and drink in the local color by myself. Sometimes, but rarely, Colin accompanied me on such mornings, but most of the time he stayed in the studio apartment and let me pick through the early day by myself. He said that he couldn't stand to be immersed in so much after-hour clutter, Santa Monica being what it was. He said also that too many gay men in West Hollywood looked alike in harsh morning light, and he was right, of course. The pallid and sunken cheeks, the quick and eager glances over-and-around carefully positioned sunglasses, the slightly-parted lips curled to crease a false, ecstatic smile. They looked alike, this horde of men. They all had something in common, too, something that made them all recognizably hopeless and desperate, but I could never quite name it to myself. Perhaps they were running from actions too difficult to admit, under the sway of some form of guilt—I cannot be sure. But I do know that guilt has a way of transforming people into something unrecognizable.

On one particular Sunday, I began to wonder if I, too, would be taken for one of these men while I walked the morning among them, if I was as unrecognizable and flat to them as they were to me, and I became resentful of being reduced by such static perception because I was surely better-off than these men.

I had allowed myself to love again.

But as I kept along the boulevard towards an uncertain destination, I began to sense more and more the likeness shared by these men. After a good amount of time in this awareness, my mind began to play what I took to be tricks on me. As the men moved, their forms blurred and suddenly came back into focus. They began to walk in a kind of unison, their long strides carrying them towards me or away from me with a military precision that cut deep into my psyche. They moved like an army. The clothes they wore, surely a motley of colors, began to bleed into a gray murkiness that moved silently but surely to further swallow up my ability to distinguish one body from another. At another time I would have been able to pierce through the gray before me and identify articles of clothing for what they were—shorts, hats, sandals, t-shirts—but this morning, after the gray began to grow and swirl around me, I could only see that all these men were altered by something sinister and carnal. At another time, and on another day, I would have recognized some of these men and been able to call them by name, even, would have seen their features as separate and distinct. But today, as I continued to walk towards someplace else, their noses, their lips and especially what I imagined to be their eyes began to collect into one monstrous organ whose only function was to swallow and appall. It metabolized the light around them, around me, pulling it down into caverns measureless and infertile. It was at that moment that I realized that nothing distinguished these men from one another, nothing living anyway, and an overwhelming sense of despair began to tug desperately inside me like a dying fetus.

Then a peculiar odor took me. It scratched itself into my eyes and throat and clogged my nostrils so that it would be known to me. It sent barbs into my brain and latched itself into my consciousness because it would be known to me. Layer upon layer, regret smoked with sorrow so charred and thick that it could have no other effect on me but to stop me utterly. It would have what it sought, and I tried to resist and keep moving, but my limbs lost my commands, and I had no choice but to stop walking further along my path towards I knew not where and let the odor overwhelm me into complete inaction. After an unknown amount of time in this petrified state, I began to be able to identify the smell that transfixed me to this spot on the sidewalk. It was the odor of shame borne out of guilt, carried by inaction, even indifference. And I was immersed in it and it was immersed in me.

Without warning, I thought of Gabriel, and the night our argument sent him to his death. That night came rushing at me like gunshots, the intricacies of the exchanges, the futility of their results. For a stream of time, only bad words had been exchanged that night, words that weren't chosen for any reason other than to harm. Our beautiful space, the one we nurtured between us over long conversations about the proper stocking methods of kitchen cabinets and the trimming requirements of an English garden, all that expanse of glorious time, subsumed by words chosen to pierce and hurt. That night, that conversation, our space folded into itself and bubbled up a newly monstrous creation, and I heard myself saying "I don't care what you do," and I saw again the pained reaction my words sent across his face. Again I heard myself saying, "I don't want to be around you any more tonight," and then my determined refusal to give him the car keys, forcing him to walk the seven blocks to the bar and back home again when it was pitch dark. If only I had allowed him the keys . . .

"David!" the call cut through the thickness swirling about me. "David, that you?"

I turned and saw someone moving through the sludge towards me. A hand raised up, palm out, pink. It rose above the putrid gray, parting it as it were, banishing it perhaps, for the thickness began to recoil from the spot where the hand had raised itself above it. I yearned to be touched by that hand, anointed by it. I wanted it to come down on top of me and subdue me or carry me out and away from the infestation that had immobilized me so. And as it came closer, I began to yearn for something worthy, something recognizably human and worthy, and I waited.

"Yes, I suppose it is me."

"Well good. I can use you right now," Rachel said as her hand came down on my shoulder. "I have to buy something for Justin's party tonight, and I have no idea what to get. I thought maybe one of the boutique stores tucked in between the bars around here would carry something that would work for her highness. You always have good ideas for gifts—help me out, would you?"

"Oh, is that tonight?"

Rachel glared at me above the rim of her sunglasses and a slight smirk flashed across her mouth. "Don't tell me you forgot. Justin will kill you if you missed his party."

"I'm sure he would, yes."

"David, really. He's been planning it for months."

"Yes, I remember now. There's a party tonight. I didn't think he invited you."

"He invited me when I ran into him last week at Pavilions. Maybe he thought that if he invited me, you might actually show. Have you picked something up for him yet?"

"No," I stammered. "No, I haven't."

"Let's go in on something together. Colin won't mind, will he?"

I thought of Colin, hunched by now over the Sunday crossword puzzle that he could never quite finish. Colin, with his chiseled nose and chin, his thick neck, his round full shoulders from which extended his meticulously sculpted arm, his large, dexterous white hand gripping a pen—he insisted to fill in the crossword puzzle with pen—his eyes turned upwards as he searched his lexicon for that one word, that satisfactory configuration of letters. I wanted to run home, my legs now free of what had transfixed me to this spot. I wanted to run home and back to Colin and have him tell me that we were alive, that we had nothing to be ashamed of and that we were both happy.

"I don't think Colin has given Justin's party a single thought," I finally said. "To be honest, I haven't given it a single thought either."

"Oh, you two," she said with feigned exasperation. "I see how it is. So wrapped up in one another that you can't make time to even think about the rest of us. I'm still technically your roommate, David, even if you haven't been home for more than ten minutes in months, and I haven't heard one peep from you all week. Not one peep."

"I know, Rachel. I'm sorry. I've been bogged down with papers to grade—I'm teaching this summer."

"Papers and poetry, that's always the tenor of your excuses these days. I swear," she said as she began to move me down the block towards a clothing store on the corner. "If I didn't actively keep this friendship alive by intentionally injecting myself into your marital bliss every now and then, it would die forgotten by you. Like a withered plant."

What happened next is something else that I cannot fully explain. I know logically that what happened next couldn't really occur, and yet, as I stand here overlooking the sea, I can't swear to myself that it didn't happen. In fact, pressed as I am against the balcony rail with the cabin and its heavy truths behind me, I suppose I must admit now that it did happen.

At that moment, I saw Gabriel. He appeared leaning against a tree that grew out of the sidewalk not ten feet from me. He was wearing the last outfit I had seen him in, that night I insisted he go clubbing without me, that night I argued with him with cruel intention, that night he was killed by a drunk in some beat up Camaro. There was blood on his clothes, splattered, across the front of his shirt which was a cool blue color. He always liked to wear blue since the color brought out the same color in his eyes, but his eyes also held specks of green in the right light, and I never told him but I preferred the green when it came. He stood there, leaning against that tree, looking almost as if he were alive, except for the blood and his hair that had been matted by the muck of the street where his body rolled over and over until landing still in a gutter. His body trembled a bit where he stood.

I took a step closer to him, leaning as he was against that tree, and suddenly he straightened up as he saw me and his entire presence became something even more fantastic. His skin began to glow a warm color, and his clothes became a shimmering of white. Somehow I knew that what I saw, this being of light, was also still him, still my Gabriel, standing right there on the corner closest to where Rachel continued to talk at me about gifts and packaging. His face was calm, serene even, and his lips were slightly parted as if he had the intention to speak to me. He wore nothing on his head, and his hair, now curls of blonde magnificence, fell to caress his thick white neck. He seemed to be standing against a slight breeze since the edges of his garments and the ends of his hair flickered and pulsed as if by wind—or maybe it was due to some electrifying energy. Glancing down, I saw that he held an open book in his left hand. The writing was illuminated by some sort of otherworldly light, and I could see that across the top of the page open to me there appeared two words in gold cursive, *Sacré-Coeur.* I couldn't make out any of the other words on the page since they were considerably smaller in size, but I knew that they were just as significant and that I would be amazed by them if I had read them.

"David."

And then in his right hand appeared a delicate glass filled with a bright and viscous liquid. The liquid seemed to move inside the frame of the glass, and somehow I could tell that it had a sort of sentience, that it was in some way alive. Perhaps it was life itself, cured from forgiveness and redemption. He extended his right hand then as if to offer the glass to me but I was too shocked by his sudden and distinct appearance to say anything to Rachel to get her to step aside and loosen her hold on me, so I couldn't move close enough to take the glass he offered me.

"David."

So, I just stood there eyeing him for as long as I could bear. I watched him watching me closely as Rachel tugged harder and harder at me to lead me out of the blaze of light surrounding me there on the boulevard into the dimmed activity of the day.

"David!"

When I turned back my stare to that spot against the tree under which he had appeared, Gabriel was gone.

* * * * *

I told Colin about meeting Rachel on the street suddenly and how she reminded me about Justin's party, and Colin insisted that we go buy him a present of our own. I didn't say anything to Colin about seeing Gabriel appear before me—how could I? I'd have to tell Colin all about Gabriel, and since I hadn't really done this, telling Colin about Gabriel's apparition seemed to me at the time to be a mistake. I kept the visitation to myself and, instead, Colin and I returned to the boulevard in search of something fitting to give as a gift. As we walked, Colin reminded me that in the invitation that Justin had sent to us, he insisted that we buy him "an expensive gift worthy of a queen" and bring it to his fortieth birthday party that he was throwing for himself at *Cirque Fantastique*. I didn't really want to go, especially when the glittering invitation arrived addressed to us with an expressed wish that we leave Rachel at home, but as Colin reminded me after I initially refused to go, if it hadn't been for Justin that first night in *Ici*, then he and I may never have met, may never have stepped so fully into each other's life, may never have steeled ourselves against the city in which we loved and lived.

At first, back out on Santa Monica, I began to panic—I half-expected more ghosts to rise and meet me, especially as we got closer and closer to the tree. But in time, we moved past the tree and there was no one and nothing leaning against it. Nothing but the tree grew there.

It didn't take us long to find something appropriate to buy. We stepped into a popular shop that offered trendy clothing and bought Justin a garish red shirt. We told him in the card that we attached to the present that we deliberately chose the color red to bring out his continually bloodshot eyes. I think Colin thought we were trying to be clever, but I really insisted on red because I wouldn't allow Colin to buy Justin anything in blue—or green.

* * * * *

As soon as we entered the shop, Colin went immediately to a discount rack and began thumbing through the clothes he found there, occasionally pausing for a moment on one or two of the garments to scrutinize it further to see if it would work for someone like Justin. I went to the other side of the floor and started handling some baubles that hung in clusters from a small standing rack on a counter near the register. My fingers passed from one necklace to the next, but nothing stood out to me.

"Can I help you find something?" The question came at me from behind. I turned to see a thin well-groomed man in his mid-twenties smiling at me with a plastic look on his face. I didn't respond to his question before he added, "We're having a sale today on all lubricants."

Here stood a typical sight in West Hollywood. Here was this slim guy, a naturally attractive guy, who had allowed the city to shame him over his thick eyebrows, now arched and thinned. Under normal circumstances I wouldn't have taken any more time out of my day to entertain such a person. Or, at best, I would've passed by such a person without paying much attention to him. But there was no getting around him now, this perfectly made-up man, who had managed to plant himself in front of the counter at which I stood.

"We're in here buying someone a birthday present," I said in a manner as pleasant as possible. "I'll let you know if we see anything that will work. The birthday boy is particularly—particular."

"Don't I know the type," he said with a smirk on his face that didn't leave any room for doubt. "Well, I'm here to help if you need any suggestions," he added and then moved off towards Colin. When he got to where Colin stood, I noticed how the salesperson's face burst into a *hey-I-know-you* expression as soon as he recognized Colin as one of the bartenders from around town, and this must have given the Versace-queen some kind of permission to be extraordinarily familiar with my beloved since he extended his thin arm and placed his limp wrist on Colin's thick shoulder, which irked me, but his eye-brows soon reset themselves into their customarily defensive arcs as soon as he realized that Colin was not interested in striking up a friendly conversation with him for some reason. After the uncomfortable exchange, I saw Colin interact with him in much the same way as I had myself, curt and somewhat dismissive, and their conversation came to the same end.

Just then Colin left the employee and made his way towards me with a couple of shirts in his hands, one a deep red with rhinestones on the collar, and the other a pale blue made of a fabric that had a kind of sheen to it that caught the light as if it had been dusted with fine glitter.

"These could work—neither one is on sale, though."

"Let's go with the red then."

"You sure?"

"Yes. The red, definitely."

"Aw-righty," he said and then turned to put the blue one back where he had found it. I motioned to the hawking employee that we were ready to pay for the item, and the plastic person moved quickly towards the register up front. I stepped up to the counter and stood across from him for only a moment before Colin was at my side with the red shirt.

"Nice choice," came the employee's voice, "that shirt is really fresh, like, literally—it came in yesterday. The entire line sporting rhinestones came in from somewhere exotic—definitely overseas. He'll love it. You know," he said, now redirecting his salesmanship towards me, "One of the necklaces you were looking at earlier would go nicely to compliment the collar line."

"That's okay, all we need is the shirt."

"Okay. But what about for yourselves? I always find that buying something for myself whenever I buy someone else a gift makes the present that much more enjoyable."

At this point, the employee's pushy attitude really began to bother me, especially since he had taken such liberties with Colin just moments before, but Colin scrunched his mouth up and bit into his bottom lip slightly. I could see my beloved's mind working, considering the employee's advice, and without too much convincing Colin was ready to act out of complete self-absorption, and would have too, if I hadn't interceded.

"I suppose I could buy something for myself—some new top for work perhaps," Colin said as he began to make his way back towards the clothing along the far wall.

"What are you talking about? You wear short sleeved muscle shirts to work—sometimes just a tight-fitting tank top. There's nothing here that would work for you behind the bar."

"We do have swanky tank-tops," came the high voice from the register, "in the back of the store, bottom rack."

"You don't need another tank-top, Colin."

Colin made a sound to express his disappointment, but he knew that I was right. Since getting his job a few months ago, Colin never seemed to run out of something new and form-fitting to make himself as attractive as possible in the well.

"I suppose you're right, as usual," Colin said quietly.

We had the red rhinestone shirt rung up—sixty-three dollars and some change—and I pulled out my wallet to get out my credit card but Colin made a face and waved his hand at me.

"I've got this babe. I've had a good couple of nights of tips. You get the next present we buy somebody."

It was a kind gesture, but one that made me also think about just how much Colin's situation had changed since the day he came home employed and triumphant. While we were still standing in that store, and especially in front of the now grim-faced salesperson, I thought this change in Colin's situation a good thing, that Colin had gained his independence as he had set out to do was a good thing, and so I let him pay for the present on his own. I smiled at him then, and we left the store holding one another's hands.

We returned to the studio apartment and, that evening, Colin took his time preparing for Justin's party even though he said that he didn't really feel like going. By this time I was familiar with the routine Colin followed each time we were going any place out of the ordinary. He set Pandora to some French club station and turned the volume up just loud enough so that he could hear it while in the bathroom. He then took the time to trim his fingernails and toenails carefully so that they were not showing any white. Despite the music, I heard the click-click-click of the nail-clipper echoed in the space around us nearly in time with the beat. He then lathered up his chest to shave the few hairs that grew there. When he had removed the hair to his satisfaction, he then went into the shower and washed himself thoroughly starting with the thick hair on his head, which he also conditioned. Wherever I stood in the studio, I could hear him humming to himself above the music as he scrubbed his body with a loofah sponge. When Colin stepped out of the shower to dry off thoroughly, he would be exceptionally clean. He then walked around the apartment wrapped in a towel for ten minutes doing this and that to let his hair air-dry into thick curls. He put on a loose-fitting tank-top, pulled on some tight-fitting jeans and began to fix his curls to bring out his eyes and square jawline. He was spending an inordinate amount of time on this, and I began to chastise him for it, but he ignored me and continued to fuss.

"You're not going to wear that, are you?"

Colin smirked at me through the mirror.

"What's wrong with it?"

"Well, it looks like you're going clubbing."

"It's a party, right?"

"Yes."

"Well, I'm dressed for a party."

"If you say so."

"Hey, I'm more than presentable—I think it's this tank-top that you seem to have some sort of issue with."

"If you're thinking that I dislike the fact that you go to work barely dressed and rake home a pile of tips because you're in a constant state of flex, you're right."

"Oh, stop," said Colin dismissively, "you worry too much about the silliest things sometimes. Besides, what you're seeing here is me planning ahead. A lot of people I know from work are sure to be at Justin's party, and they'll be on me to go out with them afterwards so I'm wearing something for that eventuality," and then he added quietly, "I suppose Rachel can go out with us afterwards, too, if she wants."

"If she doesn't, we can always send her home in a cab."

"That's true, I guess—as long as you stick to what you say and put her in that cab. She wheedles you, David."

"Rachel does not wheedle me."

"If you say so."

* * * * *

The three of us arrived at *Cirque Fantastique* at 8pm, an hour after the party officially began, and it didn't surprise us to find a collection of colorful people lined up outside. Justin was the type of person to invite everyone he knew to his own birthday party, even casual acquaintances, so we expected the place to be jetted through with people who knew him well alongside people who only knew him mildly. Although we fell into the latter category, it didn't take us long to get to the front of the line because of Colin's WEHO status, and when we did, we handed our glittering invitations to someone in coarse drag manning the door who glanced at them briefly and then waved us inside.

We found ourselves inside what can only be described as a very gay bordello. A large portion of the club had been quartered off with gaudy pink and gold cloth hung to lock in the area between the entranceway and the bar, and pairs of large, round, suspended sparkling objects dangled unevenly from every metal rafter across the ceiling. The overhead lighting was kept intentionally low, but red up-lighting from every corner contributed to the area's provocative vibration.

On the far makeshift wall opposite the entranceway a slide-show projected images depicting Justin's transition from prepubescence to present day *decadent*. To the left and right of the montage gyrated tight-skinned men inside steel cages wearing only perverse masks, gold and red body paint, and rhinestone-studded G-strings. The music penetrated the air with raw energy, and the high temperature encouraged some men not in cages to already stand about the space in their underwear.

A group of tables to the right side of the entranceway were covered with ripe fruit and lined with small plastic bottles of twist-top Perrier, and the corner near the coat room designated for gifts was overseen by a bone-thin person in Jackie-O sunglasses and an overstuffed speedo. Small groups of party attendees stood around cocktail tables or clustered themselves near the bar behind which three muscle boys with star tattoos just above their elbows drove the machine of drink orders coming in.

The entire room had been altered for the sake of spectacle, but without doubt the *piece de resistance* sat enthroned on his center-raised platform. Guests lined up to pay their respects to their host, and even from a distance I could tell by the way he moved his arms and tilted his head that Justin enjoyed every ounce of attention he had manufactured for himself. He wore a fitted outfit that caught the dim light whenever he moved, and a rich red robe draped from his neck over his thin shoulders down to the heels of his sling-backed feet; the entire length was lined with real animal fur. He held in one hand what looked to be an elaborately carved wooden staff that he took to banging on the dais over and over in an action that indicated he held court over the entire circus, and an actual crown made of brass sat atop his head.

As soon as we entered the lurid space, I wanted to turn around and leave, but Colin had already started to make his way towards the star-bar, and I had no choice but to follow him, Rachel in tow. Traversing the room was a slow process since WEHO Colin couldn't pass any group large or small without being stopped or grabbed and then forced into conversation for a certain amount of time. He'd turn around and make a face at me or roll his eyes to indicate that he was sorry for all the petty small talk, but I could tell by something under the expression on his face that he enjoyed the attention his presence produced. Still, he kept his hand firmly around mine as we made our way further and further into the space, that is, until an overly large man wearing an expensive well-tailored shirt and expensive fitted pants came up to us.

"Colin, whew. I'm so glad to see you here," said the man.

"Well, that's good, 'cause here I am," Colin replied. "I wasn't going to come at all, but David insisted. David, this is Francois. Some nights, he manages the club where I work."

"Nice to finally meet you," I said. I spun slightly to my left and motioned with my hand. "This is my friend Rachel."

When I turned back around, Francois had already led Colin a small distance away from me further in the direction of the bar. Francois had his hand on Colin's elbow and had his head bent low enough to talk directly in Colin's ear. He said something that made Colin laugh that fountain laugh of his that anywhere else would have aroused me but here made me feel uneasy and out of place. After a few seconds, Colin stepped back momentarily towards where Rachel and I still stood.

"Francois is going to take me to the bar. Don't worry, we'll get everyone a drink," and then he walked off with his boss towards where a lot of action took place.

Rachel touched my arm lightly.

"You two all right?"

"Huh?"

"You, and Colin."

"Sure, why wouldn't we be?"

"Colin seems to be in a strange mood."

"He's probably just unsettled having run into his boss."

As soon as I said this to Rachel, I knew she would see through the line for what it was—as me making up a reason for Colin's somewhat unexpected behavior. It was a lame excuse, and I knew it, and Rachel knew it too.

Rachel and I made our way to the platform, but I couldn't take my eyes off Colin. I couldn't even respond to Justin when he welcomed me in his way to his "aging event," as he called it. I barely heard Justin talk to me about the extraordinary problems he had organizing the affair, and I didn't pay attention to him when he told me to make sure to tip the bartenders since they were on loan from some porn outlet and expected to make a lot of cash money this evening. I couldn't focus on anything except on Colin, and the way he tilted his head to the side and laughed a few times whenever Francois would bend down and whisper something in his ear. When this happened a third time, a cold sensation began to grow outwards from the center of my body.

When the drinks arrived and Colin had his hands full at the bar, I saw Francois move to grab Colin by the elbow again. Colin turned his face towards the tall man and once again Francois whispered something in Colin's ear that at first, from what I could see, surprised him. Then a small smirk began to grow on his face, an expression I had been introduced to only lately. It meant that Colin was calculating his next move carefully. It meant that something was not quite right with the situation.

Colin and Francois stepped up onto the platform that still held Justin and Rachel nearby.

"I'm sorry Justin, but we have to get going."

"Get going where?" I asked.

"I've got to go back home to change."

"But you just got here," complained Justin. "You can't just leave—why change?"

"It can't be helped," Colin said, and then he turned to me. "Looks like Francois needs me on a station tonight as soon as possible—one of the other bartenders just called in sick."

"Francois, seriously, you perfect witch," said Justin. "Can't you find someone else to step in? You're taking all the pretty away."

"Well, I suppose he could," said Colin, "but he already asked me, and I already agreed to do it."

"How very nice of you," said Justin as he made a face and turned momentarily to greet other guests. "Really, you could have decided to be a bit more cruel for my sake."

Colin motioned to me and Rachel.

"Well, you two can stay if you want, but I have to get moving."

At that moment, Francois stepped forward into our small circle-of-four, giving it the shape of a pentagon.

"If you'd like, I can take Colin back to his place—I have to leave myself to check on some stock, and his place is just up the block from the bar," Francois said. "That way you two can stay here longer and not worry about leaving just yet."

Before I could respond, before I could say anything, Rachel spoke.

"It's okay David. You take Colin and then come back to the party. I'll be fine here by myself for a while," she said just loud enough for everyone nearby to hear. "Besides, I have Justin to keep me company."

"Oh please," Justin said. "I already had shingles this year."

I asked Rachel if she was sure, but I knew that she was sure, and she nodded yes and then repeated that she would be absolutely fine for a while by herself. In that moment, I knew exactly why she offered to stay in the debauched space without me. She must've sensed the same thing that I sensed, as if we were cherries paired on the same stem. I squeezed Rachel's hand, and she squeezed my hand back, and then I turned to Colin who was looking at me steadfastly with Francois standing just to his left.

"Well Colin, since Rachel doesn't mind, looks like I will take you back home to change out of your party clothes and into your bartending outfit—not that I see much of a difference between the two."

Once outside, I blinked a couple of times to adjust my eyesight, and the storm of the city rushed at me. Colin and I walked in silence to where we parked the car, and I couldn't tell if he was angry or annoyed or just plain insulted, but we kept silent as we walked. We were almost at the car when I saw her. A homeless woman, dressed all in dingy shades of white, from the hat sitting askew her head to the aged slippers adorning her feet, came deliberately across the street towards us, moving with that oblivious and casual air homeless people have when they traverse a busy street, and surrounded by that aura, used and hard, that insists to make a great deal happen despite the way in which the world has forgotten them. My eye was drawn immediately to her as she made her way across the street, talking to someone who didn't appear near her, and I thought for a moment that it must be wonderful to be this woman. How wonderful it must be to address the non-corporeal, to converse with it and get solutions to any problem imaginable. At that moment, she seemed—somehow—more alive than I could ever be, more vibrant, and she wore her determination as unequivocally as she wore her own skin. What strides she took across the open street!

I suppose I had stopped still to await her approach because Colin tugged at my arm and reminded me that he had to be at work as soon as possible.

She came directly up to where Colin and I stood now by the car and stepped between us as if to keep us apart. She looked about her person in search of something she believed she had lost. She put her hands into her pockets and pulled out a collection of items that seemed to be important to her, and she began to replace them one at a time after taking a firm accounting of them. Seeing this shook me, and I wondered if she knew that I registered her. I wanted her to know that I saw her, that I would allow myself to know her, if only as a phantom, because I thought that would give her some sort of satisfaction, or maybe because I felt it would give me some sort of satisfaction—I'm not sure.

Colin would have none of it.

"Now ma'am, watch where you're going. You don't want to run yourself into some trouble," Colin said.

"Watch yourself," came the homeless woman's taut reply. And then she turned to me, screwed up her face real tight and said in a voice that was only half aware of itself, "Hey, I know you from somewhere, don't I? Yes, I am sure I know you from somewhere."

"I don't think so." It was all I could think of to say to her, but it didn't seem to satisfy her, and she began to gesture towards me wildly.

"Your face. It's one I have seen before but not out here in the open, not like this. You've changed somehow," she said, then chuckling a bit to herself she unscrewed her features. "People tell me I'm a little crazy—so you probably shouldn't pay me no mind. You sure are a smart dresser, though."

"Thank you."

"A real fop of a man."

"Thank you, I think."

"You must be melting in all this heat."

"Come on," Colin said then to me in earnest. "This one's clearly deranged, and I have to be behind the bar in twenty."

As I made my way around the back of the car with my keys out, a hand grabbed my arm, and tugged.

"There's always prayer, you know."

I stepped around the homeless woman and left her outside in the sludge of the night with her determination taking her towards her next destination, her hands empty.

TWO

The next night, I was almost forced to tell Colin about Gabriel, about who he was and what he meant to me, but the conversation did not go well and nothing much was said about it.

We lay on our bed, Colin's large white hand over mine, and I began to talk, chatter really, with no intention of sharing with Colin any information about the past. All the while, I felt pressure swell against the inside of my ribs, and as my breathing became more and more labored, I found myself thinking about ways to dislodge from his physical touch. His hand pressed down on mine and spread thin my better judgment as I toyed with saying something that I wasn't prepared to say. Not tonight. Not while the wind still licked itself into all corners of my doubt.

I could've physically altered the way we were lying atop one another, breathing into each other's ears and eyes, to prevent something from being said, but how was I to prevent it? I suppose I could have stood up, pushed him off me, and quit the apartment altogether, gone somewhere else, anywhere else, but when the past insists to make itself known, it will come like a trumpet's burst, and yet—somehow—I kept all still and muted and uncertain. I felt my will struggle with the jerking motions of a common house fly as the conversation continued, and I edged closer and closer to saying something about a past best left where it wouldn't harm Colin and me. But the truth of the matter is, in the midst of that conversation with Colin, I feared saying words that I now regret having not said at all.

The conversation started because Colin asked me how I knew Rachel, and I thought it an odd question, especially considering that we had been together, Colin and me, for more than half a year. Colin's question made it clear that I had not shared with him anything meaningful about my Atlanta past. I suppose I could call it out now for what it was—I just didn't want to share the past with him. I held it back out of fear, but I also held it back out of selfishness—I kept Atlanta from him so that it would only be mine, mine and Rachel's, something that I could name only to myself under an October moon. It was odd that Colin never had the inclination to ask me about my past, really, at all, until that night. Until he asked about Rachel and how I came to know her so well.

"Well, she came with you here to Los Angeles from Georgia, right?"

"Yes," I said, not wanting to say any more.

"Why?" The question stung like an accusation.

What was I to say to him then? I could not bring myself to answer this question. For an answer to this simple and direct question that deserved an answer, I would have to drill deep, to crack and split my ribs wide, to run my fingers into the loess of my understanding and pull from inside me all things grown rank and gross. I was not ready to have my insides spill and shock so, having stitched them tight. I refused to lay our banquet table with soured wine and rotted meat. If I said anything meaningful, anything at all, then all of it would come without mercy upon me, upon us, for I would be forced to face the fact that I had let Gabriel go into the night without me, without a safe means to return to me, and that I had in all likelihood contributed to his death as surely as if I had been the drunk behind the wheel of the car that sent him into a gutter. In some way, then, I would be a murderer, and I couldn't allow such a thought to plant itself inside Colin's brain where it might grow wild, where it might spill over into the square of space we tailored so carefully. No, if I set such a thought free, it would surely create a thousand serpents to hiss inside our small Eden until life itself would tarnish and blacken, and then Colin would slip from me, and we would disentangle from each other, lost. If I admitted that I may have contributed actively to Gabriel's death, such knowledge would bite into my flesh like cobras and force me to quit Los Angeles completely for another location, another unsure beginning, or, worse, cause me to take Rachel back with me to try to re-stitch ourselves into the blackened fabric of Atlanta, something I decidedly could not and would not do. Threading backwards was not an option for it would mean that I had no control whatsoever over the way in which I shuttled myself through the pattern of my life, and while I stood there locked into silence by Colin's question, the thought that I was not in control of my own life promised a terrible annihilation.

No, I would instead use every possible skill at my disposal to abstain from engaging the matter entirely—to outright lie if I had to—just to avoid telling Colin more about the past than I wanted us to know.

Colin sensed my reluctance to respond to his question, and his face hardened slightly into an expression unfamiliar to me. Something dark took root in his expression, something unrecognizable and linear, and it frightened me. His perfect face, punctuated with a graceful and beautiful brow, began to crack and show bone beneath. His moist lips dried and his perfect teeth yellowed, and his eyes—still struggling fierce and blue—lost luster. Seeing him reduced to this, degenerated from the pure form made sanctified, caused a profound guilt to rise in me, and I wished that I was anyplace but there, anyplace but next to him, with his large white hand still over mine.

"She's not in love with you."

"No, she's not," I said.

"Then I don't understand. I mean, don't get me wrong, I like Rachel a lot, but a woman usually has a good reason to follow a man across the country, and don't tell me it's just to be your fag hag because you aren't too spectacular of a fag."

"Thanks," I said.

Colin screwed his eyes tight and cocked his head to the left. He turned to look at me closely and his hands suddenly went up to cradle my face. He breathed inward, slowly, and then outward, slowly, letting his exhale register against my cheeks, the sweetest, warmest breath I ever felt, and the light in his eyes returned somewhat though not fully. A soft sorrow lingered there still, lingered there since.

"Damn it, David. You know you can tell me anything, right? Anything at all," he paused for a second and breathed on me again sweet and sorrowful. "There's nothing that you can tell me about yourself now or about your past that will change the way I feel about you. Nothing."

A man can measure the substance of his life by the actions he takes when moments of pure clarity overtake him. Here was the moment to let the past wash out of me, finally. To let it rinse itself through Colin, through his skein of understanding and compassion and love for me and out of my life forever.

Here was that moment.

A spark ignited in my mind, a radiance that I couldn't say with absolute certainty originated within me. It was a small light, small but brilliant. It was forgiveness, and it bade me to wake from slumber, to stir my thoughts towards the fanciful, and the corpuscles of my blood began to surge. And just then, in that moment, I began to calculate: if Gabriel did truly appear to me on the street under that tree on Santa Monica Boulevard, shouldn't I take his appearance as a sign to reconcile my present happiness with the past lost to me? If I were to force the matter, here and now, by letting Colin into my past—could this not be why Gabriel appeared to me as he did? For a moment, I held onto the possibility that Gabriel appeared to me so that I could utter his name and be forgiven. It was wondrous, that spark. For a moment I told myself that I was ready, ready to let it all go from me—but then I remembered the living liquid, that heavenly life-force Gabriel had held out to me, and in the very next moment a deep sense of regret washed out the spark utterly and only darkness remained. I had not taken that drink. I had not taken what had been offered to me, and I was no closer to tasting that jeweled water. Even after seeing Gabriel on the street and having him offer it to me, I was no closer to redemption, and every part of me knew it.

I stayed silent and the moment passed without my saying anything about Gabriel and what remained altered something irrevocably between Colin and me.

* * * * *

For the next few weeks, I took to spending more and more time by myself out on the balcony overlooking the enclosed garden below. Much of the time, it was a remote space, quiet and still, but that is not why I liked it out there. I liked it out there because I didn't have to pretend when I was by myself. Inside, with Colin, my happiness with him brought me a deep sense of something unsettled, something unsaid, but then I would step out onto the balcony and look down at the tropical flowers growing below the large maple, and the unsettled feeling would pass out of me like a light wind through rustling leaves.

Out on that balcony, I convinced myself that if we kept our bodies inside the studio apartment, inside the room we now negotiated through half-utterances and waves of an arm, the raging city and its filth would not mar us. The walls, the windows, the door—all functioned to preserve us inside a circumference of deliberate and myopic vision, and we were the happier for it, no? For several days at a time we hardly left the room at all, preferring instead to lie about barely clothed watching classic movies and drinking gin. We passed a lot of the summer that way, with classics and gin, without the world. It's not that the outside world didn't register for us—how could it not with West Hollywood beating marvelous and gross on the other side of our door? But we had somehow come to understand that our domestic bubble sustained itself in isolation, and if we had to cross the threshold and venture out, we would never be long and would never meander. We would be quick out there and return swiftly to the shell of contentment that had formed around us in here, and when needed we set up barricades against intrusion with redoubled effort. It was a form of madness, I suppose, now that I think of it, to hold as true the notion that we could fortify our space against the bulwark of the world that grew like wild vegetation everywhere on the other side of the studio's front door.

For a long time, no one came to visit us, except for Rachel. Rachel made it custom to stop by every Wednesday after work to toast the pinnacle of the week with Colin and me, and then she would often appear again Friday evening on her way out to meet some friends of hers at a bar or a club. (I think she adhered to this routine to continue to check up on me since Justin's party, but I could never get her to admit to this.) But one particular Friday, the evening was going to develop in a way I hadn't expected. Rachel called to tell me that she was bringing with her a guy she wanted me to meet, and would it be okay if she and Frank stopped by to have a cocktail on their way out to dinner? I told her yes, of course, even though Colin had frowned at me when I motioned silently while still on the phone that he should put on some proper clothes because we would be getting company soon, and Rachel and the guy arrived promptly at six.

He was tall and thick with a devious look about his face, almost as if his boyishness had refused to harden itself into manhood. His hair, a raven black, was shorn tight and close to the sides and back of his round head, with longer pieces gathered on top into standing pinnacles of gel-hardened expression. His eyes, also dark, penetrated the space in front of him with a focused insistence that demanded attention. His large nose widened slightly at the tip, and his cheeks, which were plump and too soft looking, were punctuated by a birthmark close to his upper lip. His lips were full and sensual, and parted in such a way as to give the appearance of an utterance, though he hadn't yet made a sound. His skin was dark, like mine.

"David, this is Frank. Frank, David."

I extended my arm and greeted him, all the while conscious of Colin hovering directly behind me.

"My partner, Colin."

"Nice to meet you both," he said, with a voice like hot mercury.

"Hello," Colin said as he moved around me and introduced himself properly to the man at our door. "Come on in—we were just about to have some gin and tonics. Would you like one?"

Rachel and Frank made their way into the living space and soon took their place on the couch. Rachel sat close to Frank and Frank held his hands, palm down, on his knees, his thick fingers curled around his kneecaps. Watching Rachel sitting there, it didn't take long for me to understand that Rachel was decidedly interested in Frank, that she was attracted to his unresolved boyishness and that she brought him here for a calculated purpose.

Within a few minutes, we learned that Frank was a Master Sergeant in the Navy, that he had recently been stationed in San Diego but that he makes his way up to his hometown of Los Angeles often, and that he had a penchant for folk-art.

"That's how we met—in a folk-art store."

"Imagine that."

"Say, David, let me help with the drinks," Rachel said after a short pause. "You stay here, Colin—you're not on duty tonight."

"Yes, Ma'am," Colin said as he mimed a salute. The action brought a grin to Frank's face.

Rachel asked me to turn the music up a bit, which I did, and then we moved into the kitchen area, and that was when she fell to telling me in hushed tones the purpose of her visit. I had been right, of course, for I was always right when it came to knowing Rachel's mind. Rachel was interested in Frank, and the attraction was rather severe, hearing Rachel go on about him so in the kitchen that night. Frank had called her several days after meeting her in the folk-art store. Frank had asked to meet her for coffee but sat at a respectful distance from her the entire time and never once made a move towards her. Frank must have a terrific sense of humor since he was smiling or laughing much of the time; Frank wore the right kind of clothing, the kind that made his strong physique subtle unlike the peacocks of this city; Frank had a strong bond with his family, an aspect of his character that Rachel said told her all she really needed to know—yes, it was clear to me that Rachel was absolutely taken with him. She wasn't sure, however, how Frank felt about her—there had been no communication between them on the subject, and Rachel had the suspicion that he might even be homosexual.

"So, of course, I had to bring him here," she said quietly as she cut through a lime. "I want to know now if I should even bother to continue to fix my hair this nice and spend that extra time on my eyeliner. Beauty takes work, you know."

"You look very nice, Rachel."

"Thanks, but I'm counting on you to let me know if the effort will pay off—here, do you think this is enough?" She had cut the lime into six sections.

When we returned to the living area, we found Frank leaned back into the couch, his hands now pressed behind his head. The grin had erupted into an even broader expression of pleasure, and it was then that I could see his teeth were perfect and white. I imagined them biting hard into an apple on their way to expose its core, the juice from the fruit dripping down his square chin. Colin was seated on the arm of the couch closest to him, and the two of them must've shared some sort of joke because Frank's face transformed with laughter.

"Oh, I don't mind. Gay guys hit on me all the time. I'm used to it," Frank said.

"With those guns, no wonder," Colin replied.

I must've heard that incorrectly. I looked at Colin then and carefully to study the expression he held on his face. It seemed harmless enough, but I couldn't be sure. I had never heard Colin remark on the appearance of another man while in my presence, and the instance of it made me uneasy. But I had heard it correctly, I am sure I did. And once I heard it, I couldn't silence it. Even as drinks circulated and the four of us fell to chatting, his words scratched inside my mind, squirming there like a worm in an apple core. When the conversation turned to what we did for work, and Colin said that he tended bar at *Ici*, Frank immediately pointed his thick finger at him through the air.

"That's where I know you!"

At that, Colin blushed.

"I get that a lot—a lot of people come in and out of that place."

"I bet," Frank said. "You must meet a lot of hot guys—don't you find it hard to be in a relationship?"

"Frank—what a terrible question," came Rachel's voice.

"I mean," he began again, "Bartenders pick people up all the time, don't they? Most I know have serious reputations for that kind of stuff."

"Frank, really."

"Bartenders in this town certainly can get a lot of action, that's true," Colin answered. "But I'm content with my life, here with David. Everything else is . . . just the circus."

It was a good answer, a right answer, one that deflected itself into the comfort of our shared space, but for some reason it didn't satisfy me and I felt an uncomfortable heat rise out my chest. For a moment, I couldn't reason why this heat brushed its fingers along the edges of my face and into my eyes, this heat that strikes me hard like a two-by-four against the bottom of my jaw and then plunges itself deep through my eye-sockets into brain tissue. This heat that rises in me still, now, as I stand here in this well-appointed cabin staring at the sea rise and fall sending waves of white-capped water rising and falling lapping themselves steadily against the ship, a steady, constant pounding. This heat a steady, constant pounding that rises from my chest and strikes me in the jaw and the face over and over, *eternellement*, waves and waves of white-capped sea.

But then it hit me: the blush.

Why should it be that this biological reaction bothered me so? But it did. It bothered me so much that every other thought I had in my brain was erased and only the blush remained. It attached itself in my mind to Colin's earlier comment, and it burned there, and I could think of nothing else that evening but color rising along his white throat. It didn't matter that Rachel's anxiety was appeased. It didn't matter that Frank placed his arm around Rachel as she took her place by his side, once again, on the couch opposite where Colin perched still on the armrest. It didn't matter that we took the next hour or so and had the sort of conversation individuals bent on knowing each other better have.

Colin blushed.

If I had some power to deny the color rising into Colin's cheeks, to stop altogether the color from sighing up along his throat, to freeze it in mid-expression, I would have used it. If I had the power in me then and there to reverse the entire scene, to insert myself between Colin and Frank and stay there—even to deny Rachel's request that she bring this man into our apartment—I would have used it. I would have done anything to prevent that blush. I would have cut the blush out of his cheeks with a knife if I thought it would have done some good. But I was powerless sitting there with my hands folded angrily around my drink, and my powerlessness howled inside me, barking mad at the moon.

THREE

There crept into our lives something sinister as Colin's bartending job began to dictate more strictly his coming and going. I could barely sense it at first, or perhaps I didn't want to sense it at first. But after I began to notice it, it was always there, hovering just out of sight, a gray indistinct shape, continuously.

On early mornings when Colin would return much later than I expected, I would stir from sleep only to search his eyes to find nothing but a hardened sense of pride, and the gray ball would be there too, behind me somewhere, sometimes just to the left or right of my gaze. On certain of these mornings his return would cause me to lose my balance, and I would look into his face and find it a stranger's face framed by a blurred circle of gray—but only for a moment. Then familiarity, the touch of his thick white fingers, the glance of his green-speckled blue eyes, would rush in and reconnect us, and I readily placed the stranger and the gray ball inside an imaginary but solid box and locked it away inside my chest. I planned to forget it there, like I had forgotten the other truths I didn't care to know.

But then, after a few weeks of these unexpected comings and goings, the sinister sensation began to bleed its gray haze into our waking hours. We no longer discussed the details of whatever novel Colin had open on his nightstand; we no longer discussed the wide-ranging skills of my literature students; we no longer spent an hour playfully debating issues that rose out of columns of newspaper or that somehow slipped like eddies from the outside world. Our conversations shrank into mere utterances, necessary exchanges that facilitated the stark doings over the course of a day. Some days we spoke hardly at all, wrapped as we were in the now settled and swirling gray, and for entire evenings I wanted to cry out, to pull him back into the center and leave behind the silence and the gray, if not for my shame. My shame over keeping secrets from him, keeping Atlanta from him, keeping Gabriel's appearance and its meaning to myself, all of this prevented me from casting wide to reel Colin back through the gray. And this shame engulfed me, sending me down and away from his reach, even had he wished to reach me, cold and alone on the other end of the ocean now cloudy between us.

The more time I spent with myself, the more I grew restless and mute in that cloudy space, and our very foundation began to suffer terribly for it. Cracks began to show in subtle ways—I would sit a bit further away from Colin on the couch while we watched some television program, I began to cook and eat dinner without him on nights when we could have eaten dinner together with only slight effort, I began to take more and more walks through the neighborhood without him searching for something to correct my vision. And more and more frequently, I even took to falling asleep in front of a late-night movie instead of crawling into bed next to him, as if I was afraid that touching his naked form would bring all of my fears to play themselves across the surface of our skin.

It got so bad that soon after Colin departed for his last shift at *Ici,* I took to pacing around the small studio gesturing wildly into the air, mumbling strings of conversation to myself and smoking far too many cigarettes out on the balcony. To someone observing me from across the courtyard, it would have appeared as if I had slipped into a kind of insanity, with the gesturing and the mumbling and the pacing, but I knew better. It was a far too calculated reason that had brought me to this point, a reason that that had somehow failed me. I no longer had the surety of my will to control the elements revolving about me, and that night I found myself helpless on a weathered raft atop an angered and ancient ocean. Every inch of my body began to sting as if jellyfish darted dark and terrible through the spaces between the weakened planks supporting me. They came at me in zig-zag patterns I couldn't predict, making me dizzy, and as I began to tire, I began to question what right I had to believe in lasting happiness, what right I had to believe in happiness at all, given my past with Gabriel and my selfish refusal to allow Colin to know me fully, and I concluded that I was dangerously close to becoming a fiction, a collection of poses that sat askew and groundless in a remote and dark corner of a bar, just like Justin predicted in hushed tones up close to me the night I met Colin over a conversation that started with glitter. There I was, clinging to the loosening planks of my confidence, adrift and nearly senseless, crippled by a mistrust of all I had come to depend upon, a mistrust of everything I had constructed inside the fortress Colin and I labored to build secure.

That night found me pacing and smoking, and every item in the studio suddenly grew strange to me, from the photographs of the two of us that we kept in view atop every flat surface, to the no longer sparkling coffeemaker I insisted to buy to correct the current of my morning routine, to my own slack-jawed reflection staring back at me from the bathroom sink. I strained to make sense of that reflection, but the giant gray ball had formed in and around me, there in the near dark. And then, before I could stop it from doing so, it slipped from me, slipped outside my skin, and there came to be a separate self, a shadow-self that had been gestated in the summer heat of half-truths and neglect into its own terrible and tangible existence. And in that moment, in that very moment, I knew the interloper desired to eclipse me, to pull me passed all the black little eyes and down its great mouth.

A sort of chase began as my shadow-self began to mock my vain movements up and down the studio. No matter how fast I would shift away from it, its reach nearly had me. Whether I was on one side of the studio or the other, or out on the balcony, my shadow-self would be there, just behind me or above me, aping my movements and all the while coming steadily closer and closer, threatening to re-enter me and consume me from within.

After an hour of trying to elude it, I concluded that the only thing to do was to quit the studio completely, to run far from its domain and be with people and activity to brighten my mood. I had to deny the shadow its prize, to freeze it in some slant of light that broke itself still upon the dark underbelly of the world, and maybe prevent it from taking control of me so utterly.

Instinctually, I pulled my phone from my pocket and called Rachel. Surely Rachel would be able to tell, after only a few words, that I needed something desperately from her, but we chatted for a full minute before she told me that she had to get off the phone to head out with Frank. They were going to get a beer and listen to a local band that was playing at some dive up Ventura a way, and she didn't invite me along so I didn't press the matter. Despite my better judgment, I ended the call and stayed there in the studio, the shadow now monstrous and gross beside me, and there I was, helpless and unwilling to press Rachel to rescue me this time from the sure misery of its embrace.

* * * * *

The last night I spend on the ship, I dream. Inside one of my dreams, I hear from some distance a clamor of bells, and I suddenly find myself within an ancient album filled with images only a prophet might understand. In one of these images, I see a small boy with blonde hair dressed in a red robe sitting on the ground to my left playing a flute. Despite his age, he produces an old melody, soulful and deep, and I recognize it because it is a tune that had been written for me and me alone. The boy's hands work busily up and down his instrument, sending note after note into the air about us as the atmosphere grows heavier with each successive measure. And just before the entire scene turns to steel, the notes open another frame to me. I look and witness far ahead a large gathering of men, columns of men, who have collected themselves to celebrate something good and knowable, a mass of movement marching towards the rising sun glimmering above a great sea. And erupting from this collection of men comes a steady clamor of cheers and laughter that beckon me to join their parade, to make my way into their midst, surrender myself, and become one with the procession. But as much as I try to do so, I can't move my legs to leave where I stand and march with them in their spectacle of joy. At first I think it must be the boy and the sounds of his flute that keep me inert, the melody is that arresting. But then I look down at myself and see that I am wearing no clothes, and that all the men gathered ahead of me singing for the new day's approach are dressed in wondrous fabrics both blue and white, and I feel suddenly ashamed of my nakedness, as if it is something I had overlooked in haste, and I would turn and run but by this time the flute's song transforms my legs into tree trunks that root themselves into the spot where I stand as the melody's solemn notes lift themselves above the laughter of the parade threatening to suppress it and all promises utterly.

Then I have two more dreams. The next dream is abstract and defies my ability to understand it in any way except to know it as a feeling. My limbs have been restored to me, but I have no course to travel. And then something strange begins to fill the space. There comes at me swirls of darkness and points of light that gleam their brightness through the surrounding gray haze. And then suddenly a square of canvas opens before me, and I must be painting on it because what was once white space now fills with reds and crimsons that bleed texture and cadence into every crevice of its linen. There is something otherworldly and beautiful in its design. That is when I notice my own hands, which have been fused somehow into the handle of the brush, and I realize that what drips from its bristles is my own blood. I thrust my hands forward to spread another layer of myself thick and powerful upon the square in front of me, to insist that I leave an impression of myself, something pure and lasting, behind me . . .

I wake and find myself alone, still with a lingering desire to create, fully clothed atop the bed in my cabin and still a bit drunk from all the alcohol I had continued to consume after Catherine had left me the night previous for better prospects. For some time, I lay there unmoving, trying to think of some meaningful way to execute the dream in the world before me, and this brings with it a feeling that approaches relief, as if some great burden suddenly lifts.

That's when I look out the sliding door to the balcony and witness the pale streaks just beginning to break across the Mediterranean, sending an assortment of colors up the horizon to indicate that the night was nearly over and the dawn will come.

* * * * *

The night Colin died, I tried one last time to change the outcome of what I have always understood, especially then, would be a total loss. In our bedroom, I picked up the framed photograph of the one of us laughing under the South Beach sun, the one I perpetually kept on my nightstand. I got down on my knees, photograph in my hands, and put my back up against our bed and stared for a long time at the image of those two happy and intertwined souls. For a short time, I convinced myself that the worst was imagination, that Colin was still mine, forever mine, and that he would never cast stones heavy and deep into our ocean to disturb our universe. I recounted his words and told myself that he had good reasons, sound reasons, for coming home late night after night—the firing of a bar-back; an eruption between Versace queens; an unexpected visit by some mild celebrity—all of these seemed possible, even probable for a bar situated on the corner of Santa Monica and Robertson. For a short time, with my back up against our bed, I willed myself to accept these—excuses.

But then came the heat.

And then there was that blush.

It was with doubt heavy on my shoulders that I made my way, just over a week ago now, at midnight to *Ici* to surprise Colin at work. I figured I would show up with a smile and some tender words. It was raining outside. The streets were slick from the rain as the smog fell out of the air dense as pellets, sharp even. The drops were heavy as they fell about me and splashed against the movement and motion of our City of Angels. I walked briskly with my coat pulled up over my hair, no umbrella. The *masse ennui* picked their way through the night despite the wet, or perhaps because of it. It moved with a collective force of its own that challenged the bullets raining down on them from the vaulted sky, and it would have shuffled me into any number of corners of the street had I not been walking briskly and with purpose. I was visiting Colin at work to surprise him.

There was the usual long line outside which I bypassed by walking straight up to the entrance to speak with the guy in the headgear measuring patrons. A few insults came at me as I skirted nearly into the club ahead of the soaked faces determined to be seen even on a night like this. I didn't recognize the bouncer, and he held up his arm to block my entrance.

"I'm David Russo—I'm here to see Colin Hunter."

The guy with the headgear smiled at me with a mixture of amusement and surprise.

"So you're David. Nice to meet you finally."

"Why is that?"

"Well, Colin talks a lot about you."

"What exactly does he say about me?"

"Don't get all riled up, dude. You have that one tethered so tight, though. Haven't you ever heard of sharing?"

I didn't know how to respond to this. If the words had come from someone I had known for a long time, someone I trusted, Rachel for instance, then they would have carried weight. They would have meaning. I might have even found them amusing if they had been delivered over a couple of rocks glasses. But as they were, coming at me as they did from this stranger—a bulky, handsome stranger younger than me by at least a decade, a stranger standing in the rain outside this place where men come and go talking of Michelangelo—such as they were, these words rang hollow and dangerous. I had come here to get what was owed to me, what was mine and mine alone, and no part of me felt like sharing, not even a handshake.

"Is Colin inside?"

"Yeah, sure, go on in—back bar. He's on the left service station as usual."

"Thank you," I said as I hurried inside in front of the tight hiss that came behind me out of smog and rain. I didn't get three steps into the club when I heard my name come from half-way across the room.

"*Daa*vid," Justin raised a hand with fingers bearing overstated pieces of cut glass in motley colors. He pointed and began to shake one at me. He was practically yelling. "You've been holding out on me, *mon chere*!"

And within moments he was facing me, here in this place, again, facing me and mocking me with the ridiculous smile only an LA queen could wear without effort. The limp wrist, the colored cheeks, the linen shirt and checkered pants, the overstated buckles on his shoes, the hair now teased out in various directions with a deliberate and excessive hand. He looked like a fruit basket that had passed itself through a kaleidoscope. I could tell right away that Justin had not changed much in the month or so since his party, except his face looked even more gaunt. He must be one step closer to death, and he wore more colored bits of glass on his hands and neck to distract everyone from that fact.

"I'm sorry Justin, I can't stop now—I'm here to see . . ."

"Your blonde bartender, I know," Justin slurped on the straw plunged into his drink. "And that's precisely what I'm referring to. You know how the hive talks. Buzz, buzz."

"Buzz, buzz. Right." I began to feel grotesque and uncomfortable—I knew people talked about me, talked about me and Colin, but to be told that to my face blistered me. To be told to my face that we were being talked about, and in this place, this hive where flesh and desire serve themselves together night after night honey thick over ice. I felt a wave of panic shoot over me that nearly made me step back and out of the club, back into the rain and the smog.

"Oh, there is quite a buzz buzzing, believe you me."

Something in Justin's affectation changed. It took on a belligerence that hadn't been there before. His right fist moved to sit squarely on his hip, and his left foot in that ridiculous shoe began to tap incessantly. His cheeks sunk in even more as he puckered up his lips into a sort of scowl, and his right eye squinted slightly. Passing across his face there appeared an expression of determined cruelty; yes, I am sure of it—cruelty.

"What do you mean?"

Justin put his tongue into the corner of his mouth and turned his eyes upwards. His face froze in this unusual expression for a few moments, and I could practically feel his mind working, trying to determine the most painful way to tell me whatever it was that he wanted to tell me. I knew that he was going to say something absurd, surely, for Justin was a clown, standing in front of me, here, again, with his buckles and baubles. But fear rose in me nonetheless, fear mixed with rage, and the music suddenly changed and pulsed harder as red lasers began to crisscross the space around us.

"Well, I hear your boy is already the owner's new pet."

"What do you mean, Justin."

"Oh, just that the two of them sit and have a drink every night after Colin gets off shift, and then they run out together—into the heat of the city—to play somewhere else, somewhere up the street—perhaps at another bar, perhaps not."

I grabbed him by his sequined collar.

"Don't talk about us. I don't want you to be here in this place and talk about Colin and me, do you understand?"

He snapped back into composure, raised his left eyebrow slightly and pursed his lips together even harder.

"It's already too late for you, David."

I don't remember hitting him, but I must've because the next thing I do remember is being escorted outside quickly by Colin holding my wrist tightly. Once outside, we brushed past the line of hopefuls waiting to get into the club. Their eyes penetrated us as we walked, their lips moved and made sounds that reverberated in and out and throughout the collective of earholes that knit themselves tight-stitched around the entrance to the club. In that moment, I hated them all so completely, and I imagined what it would be like if I had been carrying a machine gun, what it would be like to create another apocalyptic story for the newspaper to jolt the world the following morning.

Colin led me up towards Santa Monica and away from the club's entrance. The night was darker, then, with rain that bit into my scalp and cheeks and stung the tip of my nose. I couldn't keep my focus on anything moving around me for too long because a mist of gray had descended. Heat swelled off my chest, rolled itself against my jaw, my head began to pound, and the pounding echoed inside my chest cavity. I became aware, then, of an overwhelming amount of noise in the grayness around me that swirled about me with sounds that spun me and made me spin uncontrollably into the gray. It would have knocked me over completely if I hadn't been held deliberately by the wrist. The tight steps we took toward that corner, with Colin holding my wrist, holding it hard, pushed us through the cacophony of gray about me which continued to stream at me as if a radio played itself out over several channels at once. When we had reached the corner, all of the sound and activity stopped together, and only Colin's voice came at me clear through the wet night.

"Do you hear me, David?"

"Yes, I hear you."

"What the hell were you thinking, punching Justin in the face like that?"

"I'm not sure. I wasn't thinking."

"That I believe—you certainly *weren't* thinking. You're lucky if he doesn't press charges," and then he paused before his face turned fully into the gray. "God damn it, David, I work there—I *work* there. Don't you get it? You can't come charging into the place and cause this kind of scene. Honestly, David, what the hell came over you?"

We crossed the street then and made our way down Santa Monica for a time, our hands no longer clasped. We walked side by side passed a packed club with its engorged front bar, passed hundreds of knowing black little eyes. All these black little eyes, they followed us just like before, and now I had a distinct feeling that every pair of them knew what I was soon to learn. They had already figured that something as delicate and rare as Colin and me wouldn't survive for long on a street such as this. Our glow was too unforgivably hot. It had to be dampened, had to be reduced to nothing more than a smolder. It had to turn, to be beaten down into cold steel, and then it would be allowed to continue to exist in that form only, muted and cold. As we walked past them, I could see how each pair of black little eyes contributed, deliberately, to this transformation. They wanted to take what we had from us so that they could peer into mirrors at the end of the day and see something less hideous staring back at them night after night, and in that moment I had no choice but to hate everything and everyone.

And then for some reason, I laughed.

"You're impossible David."

We crossed another street and stopped under the awning outside a coffee shop. People were clustered, crowded under the awning with us to escape the rain which had decided to come down now at an angle and much more aggressively. These people, they pressed all around us in the space, with Colin and me in nearly the center of them all, my head feeling like it would burst and send fire in all directions. These people, they were close to us but too wrapped up in their own wetness to pay attention to what we were doing, too focused on their attire to pay any attention to me, and yet they still drained us of all the life we had. The city pulsed and puckered about us, a hideous and insatiable asshole, and we just stood there, still, inside it, letting it pulse and pucker, letting it take from us all that had been rare and delicate.

"Are you going to give me an explanation?"

I looked at him then, and that's when I realized that he was still in his bartending accoutrement. He looked ridiculous standing outside under that tree. That tree. Colin wore a long jacket, my raincoat—I must've given it to him—over a skimpy and deliberately torn tank-top. A bandana around his head glowed a pale neon orange, and he wore matching wrist wraps and go-go shorts—all neon. His large masculine white feet bore nothing but flip-flops. More of him was exposed under my raincoat than was protected by it, and his thighs and leg hair glistened with wet despite the awning's overhead, and I am sure he must've been cold given the unusual temperature and the wetness coming down around us, but his eyes were on fire.

"Justin said something."

* * * * *

I remember that everything around us seemed to be moving slowly and darkly, as if beneath the sea. People and colors blurred passed us, above us, around us, and with complete indifference, and the time we spent in that space could have been hours, days—there was no measuring time as it gnawed pieces of us away. Our life together, once tended upon as a newborn, had dried up into something lifeless and dead, and all that was left to provide meaning were images born of fear—a withdrawn hand, poorly placed age spots, loneliness. We were no longer immune. The city had infected both of us to the core because here we were, standing on top of one another under an awning on Santa Monica, but two people had never been so far apart. We had become two people far from what they once were to each other, and I saw no possible way back.

"He means nothing to me, David."

He kept talking, speaking words that were meant to calm me down, to assure me, but through the words I could see Colin's face harden into stone before my eyes. I had become a basilisk. The skin toughened and became thick. It began to give in secret places, began to show fault lines contrary to its superior design. The more he spoke, the more that came out of his mouth, the more

I couldn't understand what he was saying. The light in his eyes began to extinguish itself, his flesh crumbled from his cheeks and fell away exposing the naked skull beneath to the air about us now thick with electricity. It was a strange yet intimate experience. The full lips that I had labored over, languished over, now turned inward, and flooded with sorrow. It became the stranger's face—there, in the rain, outside under the awning of the coffee house by the tree—and I began to ride waves of such wretched guilt carried aloft a tempest of anger that I suddenly wished it was indeed a stranger's face that I peered into, and that I could run from him, and from everything that kept coming through his cankerous opening. Nothing could have prepared me for the transformation I was witnessing, for the way it would reach inside me so and yank me hard.

We walked back to the studio apartment in silence. The rain continued to come down, but there was now something sorrowful in the way it splashed itself against the concrete. The drops themselves seemed weaker, their sting had been replaced by regret, and the regret enveloped me and transported me backwards in time and forwards in time simultaneously. I saw Gabriel's body broken and abandoned in the street, and I saw Colin as he would slip from me. There were no distinguishing marks between them now; both faces held the same sorrow and the same pain.

When I got to the top of the stairs just outside the apartment door, I turned on Colin and called down to him words bitter and unkind. I used words whose only purpose is to harm, and that was when Colin rushed up at me.

Colin moved towards me with the determination of a python. His eyes shrank into slits, black slits that gleamed in the harsh stairwell light. He would have it, this rage. He curled his large, white hands into fists that meant to break themselves against my body. He came towards me, climbing the stairs two at a time. He was a tall man, tall and large, and he filled the stairwell with fangs of anger. His white fists like cobra's heads swung at me under the glare of the stairwell light. Then he was nearly on top of me, his voice hard in my ear. The cobras hissed and bit at me. This man who loved me swung his hands at my face as he took the remaining stairs quickly to land the cobras to bite into my cheeks, one left, one right.

And then he froze.

Colin slipped forward, towards me, and I saw for a moment a look of surprise flash across his face. He lurched forward because he slipped on the wet stairs upwards toward where I stood atop the landing by the studio door. His face suddenly changed to hold the expression of a boy who knew he had done something foolish. His fist opened and his hand, his masculine, white hand went out for me to steady him, to give him balance. He reached for me, and in that instant when instinct should have moved my hand to steady him, I moved my arm down and away from his, and stepped back. I let him fall first forward and then backward, over and over, all the way down the stone stairs, until his body came to rest, crooked and broken, at the bottom of the cement stairwell not far from the street gutter.

* * * * *

Colin's life left him with a cracking and a rush; there was no shrinking of breath, rattling of rib cage, or slow closing of eyes. No fluttering, no pauses. All at once, with a giant crack as his face and upper back connected with the ground, his life ended like the sudden crumpling of an old, dried-up newspaper pitched into the hottest furnace. Just before his body made contact with the cement, there had been so much distempered motion, so much chaotic movement. The clamor and clanging of limb and skull against stone and metal as his body thumped and smacked the stairs and handrail, his finger bones grabbing at stone and steel, his shoulders and neck twisting backwards and his coming to sudden stillness face-first against the strong pavement. All at once, the air began to thicken and blur around his form as it lay there unmoving; it thickened and blurred with grief over one so fair lost. The air thickened, blurred and then resolved itself into a sharpness that tore down my throat and pierced my gullet with a raw edge like a fish's spine. And then, all at once, there he was again. Standing above the crumpled body of this man who had loved me, Gabriel held one hand up pointing towards the sky and another hand down pointing towards the earth where Colin lay. Gabriel appeared again to me, here like this, Alpha and Omega. A ring of glowing points of light in the shape of tiny stars crowned Gabriel's forehead and his eyes glowed hot and white. I saw a serene expression on his face, one that I would expect to see on an enlightened one or a Buddha. Perhaps there was some comfort to be had in that expression, but it didn't reach me. That was when I sensed the colors merge before I could see them; red and blue pooled together and swirled into a steely black that crept along the steely arteries of cement making shimmering patterns in the gray.

* * * * *

What came next was more reaction than action, more compulsion than decision. I told myself that I needed time. Time to sort out my past and my present, my past from the present, and I couldn't do that here in West Hollywood because there would be too many people asking questions and wanting answers. Once again I had to leave where I was, to turn from what was placed in front of me, what I had caused to be put in front of me.

I entered the studio apartment and stale air squeezed past me into the stairwell behind. The light from the entranceway sent an eerie light across familiar objects—the sofa, the corner of our bed, the bookcase. I didn't bother to turn on the overhead but instead chose to work stealthily in the nearly darkened space. Like a criminal, I moved from place to place about the studio picking up small objects as they came into my field of vision—my phone, my car keys, some cash I had secreted in a drawer—and stuffed them into my pockets; I reached under the bed and pulled out the small suitcase I knew Colin stowed there. I packed hastily not knowing for sure where I was going to find myself. I needed to think through the actions of the night in some place remote and away from the thousand black little eyes and their insatiate ears that would surely pin me to the back page of a newspaper should I stay. I needed more time. I threw anything that was mine near me into the suitcase, zipped it closed and ran down the stairs, stepped carefully over Colin's still body, and hopped into my car.

I hardly remember driving, but somehow I did and then up through the entryway and knocked hard at Rachel's door. When no answer came, I knocked again this time with more urgency.

After a few more minutes, the door finally pulled open and Rachel stood there in a nightgown of peacock satin, her raven hair pulled up away from her face fastened by a smart pin. With her hair pinned up and back off her face, her bovine eyes ran across me, up and down.

"David, I was in the middle of a strange dream. Two men were standing over me poking me with odd-shaped instruments and talking to each other in some foreign language that I think was French but I couldn't understand a word despite all those college courses—I'm not still asleep am I? God, you look like hell."

"I'm sorry Rachel, but I'm going away for a while, and I wanted to let you know before I left."

"It's the middle of the night—where are you going?"

"Just away."

She frowned then and I could tell that she didn't want to accept my equivocation, but I couldn't give her a more exact response because I didn't fully know where I was headed. All I knew was that I needed to leave immediately and go as far away from Los Angeles as possible, somewhere remote, somewhere no one would recognize what I had become, what I was. This one time, Rachel would have to accept my ambiguity because it was all I could offer her.

"Is Colin going with you?"

"No, he's not," I replied without thought and then turned to leave her there staring at me, but she reached out and held me back with a tender grip on my arm.

I turned back to face her. There was no way I could lie to Rachel, the one person who has always seen through me. She saw through me then as I stood in her doorway not wanting to say a word about what had happened. I didn't have to. She knew that something terrible had happened, yet again, but this time whatever happened had changed me in a way that denied her reach. She knew that I had to go, to leave and try to come to terms with it all, and that this time—this time demanded I make the trip alone.

"You will call me, right David? You will call when you get to wherever it is you are going, okay?" And she pulled me towards her, embraced me for a moment, and then she let me go.

* * * * *

I have lied to myself over and over since the stairwell, just like I have lied to myself over and over since Gabriel's death. I have played the actions of that last evening with Colin over and over in a variety of configurations screened privately inside the curvature of my skull, dramatic all: Colin drunk with rage. Colin angry over potentially losing his job. Colin overcome with desperation, overcome with jealousy, overcome with madness. I gave each of these manifestations a complete backstory of possibility, a full and convincing reason to believe them to be the truth—but in none of these did I have the strength to properly place the blame on myself, that is, not until the ice that melts in my lonesome cabin resolves itself into a dew.

I suddenly remember the vagabond who accosted me in Los Angeles, the hair mangled and wet, the walk confident. Her words resurface, and I think that perhaps if I could pray tonight, if only a little, it might help focus my mind on something greater than myself, and I might be guided into making a real choice.

It must've been during this time, long after Catherine left me to myself, and with the old woman's words still in my ears, that I slip into a kind of sleep that last night in my cabin and dream.

In the last of my three dreams, I find myself in a milk-white room with no windows and no doors and with a ceiling I can't discern up through a mist of unending space. There stands in the center of the room two thrones each adorned with chiseled bits of blue and red jewels that refract a powerful light from an unseen source high above me into rays that shoot through the mist all about like lasers. Seated on the thrones are Gabriel to my left and Colin to my right. They look perfect and whole, and I want to cry out with joy for seeing them before me so, but I have no voice in the white room under the ceiling of mist. When I approach, for I would touch them to know that they are real, each raises a hand to bid me stop my approach. So I stand still while they speak to me in a unison that informs my understanding of what I must do now that I have journeyed far to finally meet the truth as it has been made known to me here on this great ship on the sea.

I will meet the water with the full force of my body. It will feel like slamming into a stone altar that buoys me for a time while my clothes soak in the sea brine. The fibers themselves will become engorged and their heavy weight will pull me down under the water face-first. I could struggle to stay on top of the water, or I could call out for someone to help me. I could even swim for a time. But I will choose to do none of these preferring instead to allow my clothes to pull me down deeper and deeper into the cold water. When I fully submerge, I will finally open my eyes. At first I will see only blackness and depth unknowable, but the deeper I sink into the sea, the more I will begin to discern shapes in the water around me. Murky shapes, blurry and dark and still. As I pass through them all, pass beyond the dark shapes, I will travel a bit further down into the water's reach to see luminescent globes the size of dahlias appear out of the blackness below. These small balls of light will bounce towards me attached to long sinewy looking tendrils that disappear further into the deep. I will sink into them as these globes begin to beat themselves against my body, beat themselves steadily against my back, and the rhythmic movement will send me even further down into the emptiness. Soon I will be wrapped up in the tendrils themselves, tangled and twisted, as they now stretch me thinner and thinner, pulling me apart and into many pieces, and when I am nearly dissolved completely, I will then see all around me a cascade of light shimmering like a night sky of many distant stars.

And in that moment, in that very last moment, I will board the plane that would first fly me to Gabriel's grave and then to Los Angeles to face whatever would meet me there. I will then have the courage to live with myself, and to live with the angels, somewhere between the steel and the gray.

www.ingramcontent.com/pod-product-compliance
Ingram Content Group UK Ltd.
Pitfield, Milton Keynes, MK11 3LW, UK
UKHW041846190726
13854UKWH00002B/739

9 781387 803347